FALCONER'S CRUSADE

Ian Morson was born in Derby in 1947 and read modern languages at Oxford University. He now works in local government. *Falconer's Judgement*, his second novel featuring Regent Master William Falconer, is also available in Vista paperback. The third in the series, *Falconer and the Face of God*, is published by Gollancz in hardback. Ian Morson lives in Berkhamsted.

Also by Ian Morson in Vista

FALCONER'S JUDGEMENT

Ian Morson

Falconer's Crusade

VISTA

First published in Great Britain 1994
by Victor Gollancz

First paperback edition published 1995
by Victor Gollancz

This Vista edition published 1996
Vista is an imprint of the Cassell Group
Wellington House, 125 Strand, London WC2R 0BB

A catalogue record for this book is
available from the British Library.

ISBN 0 575 60079 9

Printed and bound in Great Britain by
Cox & Wyman Ltd, Reading, Berkshire.

96 97 98 99 10 9 8 7 6 5 4 3 2 1

Thanks to Lynda for all her support

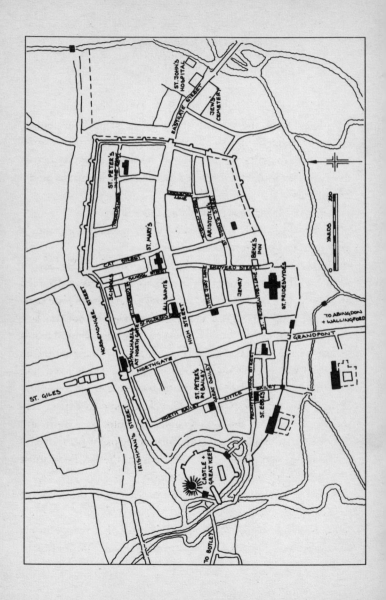

Prologue

The chill of the gloomy stone palace gripped his bones, even though this was Rome. Amaury de Montfort shivered and pulled the furs tighter around his body. Leaning across the table, he took the proffered sweet from the hands of the Englishman.

'You are ill, my lord?' asked the Englishman.

'A little cold only. Two years in a Saracen prison takes a long time to leach from your bones.'

He bit into the succulent marchpane, and the sensation of sugar and almonds caused his mouth to water. Saliva dribbled on to his beard, now peppered with grey from years of imprisonment. He shuddered again and the other man, his solemn face expressing concern, leaned forward. As the Englishman's features came into the pool of light cast by the candle, de Montfort thought he saw a look of disdain. He blinked and looked again. Now he could detect merely a mask reflecting nothing but the pomposity Amaury had come to expect. He stuffed the rest of the sweet confection into his mouth and reached for an apple. The Englishman anticipated his move.

'Take this one, Count. It is the ripest of the lot. Food must have been poor in the Saracen gaol.'

'I would not grace what we were given with the name of food. Swill was more like it.'

De Montfort began to eat the apple, though a twinge in his bowels warned him that he was overindulging. Still, better to be ill from a surfeit than from too little. The griping pain came again, more violent this time and he twisted in his hard wooden chair.

'My lord, I fear you are ill.' The Englishman's voice seemed distant and distorted. His face was ebbing and flowing in and out of the light of the candle. A grotesque mask.

'There is something wrong. Send for my physician.'

The other man brought his face close to Amaury's. He could feel the sweat coursing down his features, dripping from the end of his nose. He shivered with cold then instantly felt hot. The voice he heard was cold with hatred.

'I fear it is too late for the physician.'

A pincer of pain twisted his entrails, burning like a sword thrust deep into him. Amaury pitched forward on to the floor and the chair fell over with a crash. Surely his servants could hear the noise? He tried to call out but his mouth was full of blood and vomit, and his shout was a mere bubble.

'No need to waste your energy. I ensured your servants were well supplied with wine. They will not hear you.'

A croak escaped the throat of the dying man, which now burned with a fire equal to that of his stomach.

'Murder.'

'Merely a merciful release from the sinful material flesh of the body. I give you a release more swift than your father did mine. It is a blessing.'

His body was racked with great spasms of pain and his legs kicked out involuntarily, hitting the table. It tipped and the pottery bowl crashed to the floor, spilling apples and sweetmeats all around him – all brought by the Englishman, who claimed to know his brother and who sought to bring news to a Crusader with two years to catch up on. The stone flags pressed cold against his burning cheek. His limbs would not obey him. He

8

could merely gaze at the feet of his killer and the great black shadow he cast. His voice came again, whispery and distant.

'I dispatched your brothers long ago, but had to wait until you returned from your mad Crusade. How like your father you are.'

As he lay dying, besmirched by his own vomit, a strange clarity came over Amaury's mind and the truth echoed through his skull. His lips tried to form the word, but he died before he could say it.

Heretic.

Chapter One

The crude bird-shaped thing flipped in the air and plummeted to the ground at the foot of the tower. It splintered into pieces on the icy, hard earth. At the top of the tower, a face peered out over the parapet and then disappeared. Eventually the man emerged through a door at the foot of the Great Keep fortifying the west end of Oxford and began to cast around in search of the artefact he had launched from the tower. He walked in ever greater circles out from the yellow stone walls until his foot crunched on a piece of the debris. He sighed as he picked up the evidence of his continuing failure to emulate the simplest of God's creatures. He still could not mimic the birds' skill of flight, and he turned the hide and stick construction over in his hands. It had been a long day for Regent Master William Falconer.

He had risen well before the first hour of the day, barely six hours past midnight. In the darkness of the winter morning, he briefly splashed icy water over his face before sharing a simple breakfast with the students in his hall, Aristotle's. By then he had already taken the opportunity to finish the bird-shaped form he thought would soar and swoop from the tower when he had time to launch it. He insisted, as was the custom, that his students spoke only Latin when sharing meals. But by sext, the sixth hour of the day, after having taught his younger students in the hall and having got the main meal out of the way without too much attention to Latin, he was impatient to try out his model. However, he still had lectures to give all afternoon in schools. The ninth hour, nones, was well past before he had a chance to test the thing, and he gladly forewent supper to hurry to the Great Keep in the gathering gloom.

Now he was hungry and it had all proven a waste.

How he missed his friend and teacher, Roger Bacon, to discourse with. The outspoken friar had been banished to a Franciscan convent seven years ago, in 1257, and Falconer often felt a need to test his ideas against the man's mind. It was Bacon who had taught him that science was a matter of investigation, not playing with words. And it was Bacon who had opened his eyes to Aristotelian logic, which Falconer used to solve all sorts of problems. Including murders. Though Friar Bacon would have scorned such a curiosity as idle interest, diverting William's mind from the study of mathematics and alchemy.

Falconer had led a varied life before meeting the friar, travelling the world and seeing its wonders. He had arrived at Oxford via the University of Bologna, where he had learned from great minds, and had determined to settle down to a life of study. The quibbling, disputatious nature of the regent masters had begun to convince him that he had made a mistake, when he happened to attend a lecture by Roger Bacon. The friar was already developing a reputation as a magician, and this attracted William. Anyone who roused the envy of the narrow minds at the heart of the university must have something to offer. The lecture on the 'usefulness of nature' fired him to understand the physical world.

Although clearly he had not understood the physical nature of flight yet. Returning down the High Street of a darkening Oxford, head down against the icy wind that blew along its length, he recalled that a new student was due to arrive today. What was his name? Symon — yes that was it. He cursed that he had spent too long at the tower with his experiment. He should have been back at Aristotle's to greet him. Who knows what other Master, touting for students, might snatch him from Falconer? The annual fee of four shillings per student was welcome to supplement his frugal existence. He skipped over the freezing sludge in the centre of the road and hurried on.

Thomas Symon stepped stiff-legged from the cart down to the frozen mud. Stumbling on tired limbs, his foot slipped in the channel running down the middle of the street. The grey, turbid water slid warm over his ankle despite the cold of the evening and he shuddered to think what had been cast into the gutter higher up. This was not how he imagined his arrival in Oxford. He should have had a fetcher to bring him to the university, but he had not turned up and Thomas had had to undertake the journey on his own. He pulled his foot out of the slime and sighed. The son of a farmer, he had been lucky to be chosen for a place at the university. At least that was what his father had said: 'You should be here helping me and your mother, so be grateful.'

Thomas was grateful, but he knew his ability at grammar had shone through the mud of the farmyard. He knew the local priest occasionally sponsored clever minds to train as clerks, especially if they were from poor families. Thomas had striven hard to impress Henry Ely, and now it had paid off. He was indebted to him, and reluctantly to his father, who would never let Thomas forget the fine he had to pay to release his son from his obligations to the manor. He was glad his mother understood and was able to persuade her husband, and glad to be free of the dawn to dusk grind of the farm work. He had been forced to delay his departure until his father was satisfied no more work existed on the farm, and would now have to catch up on the other students. But now he was here. The university.

On the long and tiring journey through the troubled England of 1264, he had whiled away the time with dreams of how his arrival would be. Town folk would nudge each other and point at this no doubt brilliant scholar as he made his way down the main street. The Master of his hall would rush to welcome him, ushering him into the blazing warmth of the great communal room of the scholars, already eager to debate subjects from the quadrivium with him.

The reality in no way matched those fond ideas as the carter hurled Thomas's bundle down from his perch above. It landed with a thud at his feet and the carter whipped his horse into motion. Thomas leapt clear of the wheels as they cracked through the surface of the frozen mud. The rear one dropped into the channel of sewage and squirted filth over Thomas. His clothes already reeked of chicken droppings picked up from the hours spent on the back of the cart squeezed between wicker crates of live squawking birds on their way to market. Now the stench of human ordure was added to his travel-stained clothes. He bent to pick up his bundle and, as he slung it over his back, looked around. The cart had already disappeared into the mist. He was alone and it was dark.

Thomas had planned to arrive in full daylight and ask his way to Aristotle's hall which he knew lay between Kibald Street and St John's Street. There he was to ask for Master William Falconer. But his plan had gone awry when he reached Nuneham and found that no one was travelling north because one of the vast baronial armies was passing Oxford on its way to the Welsh Marches. It was not safe for anyone to get in the way, especially if you didn't know who to claim allegiance to. Thomas had fallen into conversation with a carter whom he had encountered breaking his journey by the side of the roadway with a tasty meal of dry bread.

'Why can't de Montfort and his cronies settle with the King and leave us poor folk to earn a crust?' grumbled the carter. 'I have no more feed for them chickens and must get them to Oxford tonight.'

Thomas too was anxious to reach his destination. He had no money to pay for a room and dreaded the thought of sleeping out in the cold overnight.

'If I spy the land ahead for you, we could travel together. And when the coast is clear I could travel in your cart.'

The carter's beady eyes sized up Thomas. He was only a lad – fifteen years of age perhaps. But he was tall, blond-haired and his blue eyes made him look strong and alert. And a second pair of hands was always useful to fight off robbers. He hawked and spat at Thomas's feet.

'Get up on the back. The first five miles is open country and we'll need to hurry to make Oxford before dark.'

Although the cart had lurched and bounced along the rutted road, Thomas had managed to doze off and woke with a start when a rough hand clutched his neck. It was only the carter.

'You'd not be much use in a fight,' he grumbled. 'I could have slit your throat already.'

'Sorry,' mumbled Thomas, ashamed at his lack of manhood. Then doubly ashamed for apologizing to this coarse peasant. Wasn't he a scholar after all?

'Let go.'

Thomas struggled in the strong, horny grasp of the man, whose grip tightened on the jerkin at his throat. His face drew close enough for Thomas to smell his rotten breath and see the stumps of decayed teeth. The man snorted and released his grip.

'Aah. You're lucky I need you. Keep your eyes open now – we have the forest to go through and I must keep my eyes on the marks.'

'Marks?'

'Have you not travelled before?' grunted the carter.

Thomas did not wish to reveal that he had not, until now, travelled more than a mile from the village of his birth, and kept quiet.

'Other wayfarers mark the trees and bushes with the safe routes. Look, see that knot there.'

Thomas nodded, though unsure what he was supposed to be looking at. Keeping his eyes peeled for robbers must surely be easier. At last clear of the forest, Thomas had his first sight of Oxford. A low slope ran up from two rivers to the clean lines of the new town walls showing yellow in the gathering dusk. They had barely made it through the South Gate before it was closed.

But now Thomas was in Oxford. Suddenly he realized the carter had left him without a word of advice on how to find his way. His feet began to feel the cold of the ground striking up through his thin soles. He shuffled on the spot and looked around. The dark houses with their shuttered windows towered over him, and the street stretched for ever into the darkness. Thomas felt alone, yet it was said over five thousand people lived in Oxford. Where were they all? There was nothing for it but to find his own way. If this was South Gate, then he should take the first turning right to find Aristotle's hall in the east of the city.

He shouldered his bundle and set off up the street, careful in the dark to look out for the dung heaps scattered along this normally busy thoroughfare. Walking north barely a hundred yards he found a narrow lane leading east; it looked even darker than the street he stood in, but it led in the right direction. Hesitating but a little, he turned into the lane. Only a short distance further on the row of houses to his right ended, giving way to a grassy waste covered with a low-lying white mist. The town walls looked almost luminous through the gloom. Imagining ghosts looming out of the mist already, he nearly dropped his bundle and ran when a black figure seemed to materialize out of the wall on the left ahead of him, then disappear into the haze.

'Hello.' Thomas's voice was timid and cracked. He wasn't too sure if he wanted a reply from the ghostly figure. But it was gone anyway and he sighed with relief. Cautiously approaching where the figure had seemed to step through the wall of a solid building, he realized it had in fact come out of another narrow lane hidden by one wall jutting out further than its neighbour. Perhaps the apparition had been human after all. Nervously, he began to whistle to reassure himself that everything was normal.

The man saw the hooded figure from behind, and the faces of the two shepherds concentrating on what the hooded man told them. It was a fixed tableau like a miracle play performed on the back of a cart. He knew the hooded man held the book in his hand, and was reciting from it. A light from the fire in their midst illuminated the two shepherds, but the third man was just a black form. Without hearing he knew the reader was speaking of Saint Peter and Saint Paul. The scene was so peaceful, he was almost lulled into sleep. But he knew what was to come, and tried to call out. His voice was just a croak, unheard above the crackle of the fire.

Then he heard the jingle of stirrup and horse armour, and turned to look behind him. The shape on horseback seemed huge and inhuman, encased in richly chased armour. The noise of the hoofs was thunderous to him. Why couldn't the figures in the field hear it? Steam snorted out of the horse's nostrils and its hoofs flashed in the moonlight. It appeared to him as some unearthly engine of war. The faceless knight on the horse's back drew out its sword with a shiver of steel.

He turned his gaze back to the group in the field, so defence-less and innocent. Once again he tried to call, but no sound came from his lips. Surely the shepherds, facing the direction of their nemesis, must see the knight and save all three men? But they were oblivious, intent on the speaker's words. The machine of war bore down on them, the sword cutting great swathes in the air, which seemed to hiss as it was sundered. Just as the horse's hoofs seemed destined to trample the simple shepherds, the hooded figure turned, his face visible at last.

'Father!'

The call came too late. The inexorable arc of the sword swept down on the upturned face and cleft it almost in two. Great gouts of blood and brain spattered over the book, still clutched in the quivering hands of the hooded man.

He came out of his trance with a cry, sweating yet cold. As with every time he relived his father's death, he strove in vain to recall if he had seen his soul ascend to Heaven. There was now no consolation for him but revenge. Rising from the chair, he resolved to silence the only impediment to that revenge. He knew his dream occupied but moments in reality, and the servant girl would not have gone far. It had been foolish of her to reveal her knowledge so openly.

At the door he peered into the night. The mist seemed to the man like myriad souls whirling around him. It would be easy to stalk the girl in it. After leaving his house, she would have turned to follow the main road. He slipped out the side door and down the narrow cut between the backs of houses on Shidyerd Street. Coming out opposite St Frideswide's he reached the corner before her, and she almost ran straight into his arms. Seeing who it was, she was afraid but subdued, unsure of how he could have got ahead of her.

He heard the whispering in his ears of the unencumbered souls, free of their fleshy tunics. They flitted silently, like owls on ghostly wings around his head.

'Where is it? I want it back.'

His question, hissed out, made the girl stagger back in shock. He knew if he turned around that he would see the armoured knight on horseback rising over him. She was afraid of it, but he was not. He had seen it too many times, heard the snort of the horse's nostrils. Still the souls of the dead writhed around him, white and insubstantial.

Through the mist there came the incongruous and distant sound of someone whistling nervously. The girl glanced over her shoulder at where the sound came from. Her eyes betrayed the hope of salvation, and a scream came to her lips. He thrust forward at her, the faceless knight at his shoulder urging him on. There was the whistle of a blade and the scream was cut off. He gasped with pleasure as the girl's soul leapt from her mouth to join the other wraiths.

Thomas had just managed to calm his nerves when the dead quiet of the night was pierced by a high-pitched squeal which died away into a bubbling silence. His heart thumped in his chest and his legs felt weak. To support himself he leaned against the wall of the building, his eyes closed tight. The rough mud plaster of the wall felt icy cold to his cheek. He realized he was sweating, sure this was the Last Judgement that the friars said was certain and not far off.

When another minute passed and the silence suggested he had been a little hasty in his assumption, Thomas cautiously opened his eyes. Nothing had changed and the dead had obviously not all risen from their graves as promised. He tried to still his thumping heart and think where the sound had come from. It seemed to have come from further down the lane in the direction the figure had gone. Thomas clutched his bundle tighter, wishing he had the sturdy cudgel his father kept in the house for unwelcome visitors. Even so, he felt drawn towards where the scream had come from. Perhaps, after all, it had merely been the squeal of a pig – somehow he couldn't convince himself of this.

He willed his legs to move and made his way down the lane. Slow at first, his legs seemed to speed up of their own volition until he was almost running. The lane twisted to the left and as he turned the corner his feet caught on a bundle of clothes and he fell sprawling to the ground.

His hands stung from the impact with the frozen ridges of churned mud, and raising them to his face he thought at first he had cut himself badly; they were covered in blood. Kneeling still, he wiped away the blood on to his jerkin and gazed stupidly at both his hands. There was no cut. Trembling, he looked by his knees at the pile of clothes. He cautiously lifted the corner of cloth and revealed the still, pallid face of a girl. The eyes stared blankly at him but no white mist of breath came from her lips.

Thomas screamed and stumbled to his feet. Crossing himself, he stared down at the girl's face. She was young and beautiful – how could she also be dead? Her brown eyes stared blankly through long lashes and her hair tumbled around the white flesh of her face. Her lips were still red and full. A few strands of hair lay across her face and Thomas felt a stupid desire to tidy them. He bent down and brushed his hand across her cheek; she was still warm. Flinching from the touch, his hand pulled back further the hood covering her neck. It revealed a livid cut from which blood still oozed, steaming in a bitter parody of living breath. Thomas was transfixed, realizing why the cry he had heard had been cut off. Suddenly he became aware of voices near by, distorted in the mist but getting closer.

'Hello. Who's there?' said one voice.

'Did you hear a scream?' came another to the left.

'Yes. It came from over here.' The first was closer now.

Some sense told Thomas that he should not stay here, standing over a body with blood on his hands. He willed his legs into motion and stumbled away from the voices, falling into a doorway and picking himself up again.

'It's there. Look, a body.'

Thomas pressed on until his feet slipped from under him in the icy lane. He crashed to the ground, his breath coming out in a great gasp. The sound was enough.

'And there goes the killer.'

Thomas looked back and saw two men standing over the girl. Black shapes outlined in the mist. They were pointing at him. He rose and staggered past an alley to his right. A strong hand clasped over his mouth and an arm wrapped around his waist, dragging him into the alley. In blind panic he wriggled to get free until stars exploded in his skull and all went black.

Chapter Two

The clanging of the Morrow-Mass bells at St John's and St Peter's in the east roused William Falconer from his sleep. A mild curse hung in the cold air as he pulled his tunic closer around him, the dawn chill still in his bones. He swung his feet from the bench where they had been tucked into the fur of his academic hood. The frozen rushes crackled underfoot and he remembered he had gone to sleep failing to ensure the fire in the hearth would last the night. A stronger curse streamed from his lips.

Falconer was a massive man whose clothes seemed to ill fit him. His wrists stuck out well clear of the frayed ends of his sleeves, ending in raw, bony hands more in keeping with a labourer than with a regent master of the Faculty of Arts. A student caught by the gaze from his pale blue eyes set in a coarse, ruddy face had the uncanny feeling that his every secret was being stripped from his soul. That look served him well on many an occasion.

As he crossed the room to the hearth it was, however, clear that his massive frame was belied by the grace of his movement. Crouching by the fire he breathed a sigh of relief when he saw a faint red glow in the ashes. Sweeping up some dry rushes from the floor he coaxed a few yellow flames from the ruin of yesterday's fire. Crouching even lower, he blew on this unpromising start and reached out blindly for more kindling.

His hands fell on the unmistakable form of a leather-bound book left on the floor the previous evening.

Turning from the fire, he lifted the book close to his face to examine it. He had to squint because those eyes which caused dread in the hearts of guilt-ridden students could see little further than the end of his nose.

'Ah. Al-Khowarizmi,' he murmured under his breath.

It was his much-treasured translation into Latin of the Persian mathematician's treatise on algebra. A present from Falconer's friend Grosseteste, given only days before the latter had died and all his books had been passed to the Franciscans.

Last night he had read part of it again before taking the late walk that was his habit. Although the streets of Oxford were said to be unsafe after dark, he knew his very size was security in itself. Anyway the quiet of the night helped clarify his thoughts as he wondered what had happened to the boy who should have arrived that day.

Last night, however, had not been quiet. First he had heard the piercing scream that sounded like a pig in the slaughter-house, and then as he ran towards where it came from he had heard the cries of people giving chase. It was then that someone almost ran full tilt into him. He instinctively grabbed the figure who struggled in his grasp and struck his head on a wall. William was about to call out when he looked down at the figure that hung limply in his arms. He was a boy, still peachy-cheeked and clearly incapable of much harm. He clutched the boy to him and pulled him back into the dark of the doorway on the corner of St John's Street.

His good sense told him that justice would not be served if the townsfolk pursuing this boy caught up with him. Too many times in the past the anger of the town had been vented on innocent students, an anger fuelled by the stranglehold the university already had over the town. His mind was racing as the sound of the boy's pursuers came closer, their cries like the baying of hounds after deer. There was little good in hiding in the doorway as the hunt would split at the junction of the lanes, testing out both avenues of escape. Boldness was required.

Falconer wedged the limp form of the boy into the doorway, gathered Thomas's bundle from the ground where it had fallen and tipped the few clothes loosely over the body. It did not bear close examination but it would have to do. He then strode purposefully towards the sound of the pursuers. He was just in time – he blocked the end of the lane just as four rough and red-faced men reached the junction. He took the initiative.

'I heard all the noise. What has happened?'

'A murder, that's what,' growled the largest of the men, his pockmarked face contorted with anger. Falconer murmured a prayer and the men shifted uneasily, clearly anxious to continue the pursuit but not daring to interrupt the prayer.

'Who is killed?'

'A woman. Down there by the corner. We saw the killer come this way.'

'This way?'

The older man of the group spoke up, his watery eyes gazing suspiciously at Falconer.

'Who might you be, anyway?'

Falconer ignored him. 'I saw no one come this way. He must have gone up to the High.'

His bulk planted firmly in the passage, he stared coldly at the group of men. The old man held his stare, but the others fidgeted, unsure of challenging this massive man who, Lord knows, could probably have them clapped in gaol if they accused him falsely. Looking over Falconer's shoulder, the old man could only see an empty lane, and a pile of clothes in a doorway. Still he was not sure. Pockmark broke the stalemate.

'Come, John. We're wasting time. He must have gone towards the High as the Master said.'

Reluctantly, old John turned and followed his comrades as they disappeared into the murk. Falconer remained where he was. He could only see poorly as the figures retreated from him. He could, however, see enough to know that the old man turned and looked suspiciously over his shoulder before the mist closed around him. He sighed in relief and wiped the sweat from his brow, which had formed despite the cold of the night.

'Lord, never let me say again that you don't respond to my prayers. Now let's attend to this child.'

The boy was still unconscious when Falconer returned to him. Quickly he stuffed the poor, homespun clothes back into the sack the boy was using to carry his worldly goods with him. A scrap of parchment fell from the folds of a tunic that he picked up, and peering closer Falconer saw his own name on the outer part of it. He would need to revise his first thought that this was some young vagabond. Indeed it was probably the young scholar he had been expecting. He had been recommended by Henry Ely, an old friend of Falconer's, whom it pleased to support poor scholars occasionally.

He looked at the still features of the shape in the doorway, then returned his attention to the letter. The hand was indeed Ely's and on unfolding the well-used piece of parchment, still bearing the trace of some previous scratchings of Ely's, Falconer read his friend's recommendation of Thomas Symon of Broughton.

Now the regent master picked up the piece of parchment from his table where he had dropped it the previous night putting the boy to bed. It was five years since he had seen

Henry Ely, but he still thought of him as a close friend. He recalled the times spent disputing Aquinas and Aristotle, both men knowing they would never reach agreement but enjoying the argument all the more for that. Henry's round face would grow redder as Falconer refuted his every point until he thought Ely would burst. And he usually did, but only in the laughter of defeat. Now Falconer was a regent master at the University of Oxford and Ely a country prelate. But the latter had a knack of finding promising lads learning their grammar and passed them on to Falconer to attempt the disciplines of the trivium and quadrivium. The seven liberal arts of ancient time were still the foundation of knowledge. The first three, grammar, rhetoric and logic, formed the basis for studying the great Four Arts of music, arithmetic, geometry and astronomy. Seven years of study were required before someone could hope to become a Master. And the supreme science of divinity called for at least another seven.

'And here is the latest offering,' muttered Falconer, looking at the sleeping figure on his bed. Thomas turned over and spilled the coarse blanket on to the rush-strewn floor. Looking back at the fireplace, Falconer groaned as he realized his attempt at reviving the fire had been wasted. The fire was now entirely dead and he bent down to pick up the blanket from the floor. There was a violent knocking at his door.

'Master, are you awake? I need to talk to you.'

The voice was that of Hugh Pett, a student of four years' standing at Oxford and now close to the rigours of testing by disputation. He was William's star pupil, though he would never admit that to anyone, least of all Hugh himself.

'Hugh. Come in.'

'Master, there's talk of a murder . . .'

As he spoke his eyes fell on Thomas's form, tossing on the

narrow bed against the wall. He turned back to the massive form of the regent master, a strange query in his eyes. William returned the stare.

'Fear not. His virginity is safe with me.'

Hugh blushed, and dropped his eyes to the floor.

'As for the murder, I know of it. Tell the rest of the hall it would be wise to go carefully today. The town will not take too kindly to cheerful clerks when one of their own is dead. Now let us rouse young master Thomas.'

He strode over to the bed, grasped the head and tipped it sideways. With a cry Thomas fell to the floor, a tangle of arms and legs and blanket.

'That is the last morning you sleep beyond the sixth hour,' warned Falconer.

Thomas stumbled over his apology, and scrambled up from the floor dusting the rushes from his tunic. His eyes took in the room which had been too dark to see properly the night before. Then he had come round to see a huge menacing figure looming over him, and had cringed away, fearing his last moment had arrived – that he was to be taken for the murderer. However, the man had calmed him with a gentle touch at variance with the rough appearance of his hands, which looked to Thomas more like the workaday hands of his father. It was then he learned he was in the safety of the very hall he had sought and that this strange man was William Falconer.

Strange man indeed. On one wall of the room was a shelf of books, more than Thomas had ever seen in the possession of one man. Yet more were strewn on the wooden table which dominated the centre of the room. The morning light filtered through an unglazed window to the right of the fireplace. The beam shone through dancing dust motes on to the end of the table where a jumble of bones lay together with the dusty grey remains of some long-dried herbs. In the farthest corner from the bed Thomas's stare was returned by the unblinking gaze of an owl, calmly perched on a rough-hewn stick wedged in the angle of the walls. Beneath it, a row of earthenware pitchers were arrayed along the floor. Thomas thought instantly about his mother's warning of alchemists and their desire for fresh bodies to work upon. He shivered.

'When you have performed your inventory of my room, I wish to introduce you to Hugh Pett.'

Falconer's rumbling voice brought him back to reality, and he looked for the first time at the young man who stood in the doorway. Pett's clothes betrayed a family who could afford to support him at Oxford. His plain black tunic reached almost to his ankles, but it was covered by a rich scarlet toga with slits in the sleeves through which his arms and slender hands protruded. His pale face was framed by long and carefully cut ginger hair, and divided by a thin aristocratic nose. Only when a grin split the solemnity of that face, as it did now, did Thomas feel comfortable. Even so, he clutched nervously at his short homespun tunic and turned away his already weather-beaten face, examining the floor.

'Don't be daunted by his pretty, mincing looks. He is quite tolerable in spite of them. Hugh, see if you can find some leftovers for Thomas – he did not have chance to eat yesterday. And keep him off the streets, I sense a riot if the town is provoked.'

As the oak door closed behind the two boys, Falconer eased his bulk into the rickety chair at the table and picked up an array of bones linked with thread. It was a bird's wing and carcass, and he began to puzzle again over its relationship to human anatomy. He drew an inkpot towards him and took up a quill, but his mind would not concentrate on the task of simulating flight. Pensively he tapped the bony carcass on his lips. Last night after the boy had come round and recovered from his shock, he had questioned him gently on the incident in Shidyerd Street. It was probable that the apparition he had seen was the murderer. But was he a mere nightwalker intent on robbery, or were more sinister forces at play? Thomas thought the figure could not have seen the girl. The mist was too thick. Therefore Falconer had to deduce the figure knew the girl was abroad and where to cut across her path. It all suggested some intent. But what?

He threw the bones down on the table with such force that the cord snapped and the skeleton fell in pieces on to the floor with a clatter. The owl's eyes snapped open and its head swivelled to take in the disturbance. Seeing nothing to further interrupt its sleep, it settled down with a flick of its wing feathers. Falconer ignored the mess he had created and left the room. He had to see the body.

Master John Fyssh had seen the body and wished he had not. He had awoken to the sound of insistent hammering at the door leading into the lane. He was unable to ignore it and had reluctantly prised his bulk off the bed and gone down the steep wooden steps, calling peevishly in his high-pitched voice as he went.

'Very well. I am coming,' he piped, pulling his fur robe tighter round his ample stomach.

He stumbled in the darkness of the passage; it could not even be dawn yet. Grumbling, he incautiously opened the door before thinking that at this hour it could be a nightwalker. He was relieved to see it was one of the town constables, then angry that such a man should disturb the righteous sleep of a regent master.

'There had better be a good reason for this disturbance, Constable.'

'Have you not heard the hue and cry? There has been a murder.'

'What business is that of mine?' Fyssh seemed unconcerned at Bullock's reason for awaking him before his normal hour.

'It is your servant who has been killed.'

Bullock was deliberately blunt, examining the fat man's face for signs of foreknowledge. Was the spasm that momentarily creased his corpulent features fear of discovery? Bullock could not be sure before Fyssh gave an angry cry, 'That bitch. She never was of use.'

He had continued cursing his ill luck, only to realize the constable was still standing in his doorway, quietly insisting that he see the corpse. It was of some surprise that he had been persuaded to do so – he was not usually so intimidated by such a common person from the town, someone with no actual jurisdiction over him. Yet this ill-shapen man had somehow survived his tantrum and patiently waited while he slowly dressed in his warmest clothes. In the end Fyssh convinced himself he acquiesced merely to get rid of a person who more resembled a toad than a human being. He much preferred the company of well-formed young men with minds to shape.

He had hastily affirmed that the corpse was indeed that of Margaret Gebetz and had abruptly turned to leave the side chapel in which she lay, half expecting the constable to continue to badger him with questions. Surprisingly, nothing was said and Fyssh breathed a sigh of relief at what he saw as his release. He left the constable washing his hands in the sacramental basin.

Coming out of the church, he had seen the bulky shape of that interfering man Falconer hurrying towards him. He was about to grudgingly give him a good-day, when Falconer swept past him without a word, his eyes seemingly fixed on some distant target. Cursing the man's incivility, Fyssh returned to Beke's Inn to face the horror of a morning without a servant to prepare his food. He also tried to reconstruct what he had done the night before. Most of it had disappeared into a drunken haze after a certain point.

The Lady Chapel in St Frideswide's was icy cold. Perhaps just as well, as it housed the mortal remains of the murdered girl. The archway from the north transept framed what seemed a reverential scene, with the figure of a man bent over the recessed basin at the east end of the chapel. To one side stood a stone cross older than the chapel itself with, on its base, carved shapes that were rounded with age. It had no doubt been moved from another, older part of the church. The figure turned and Falconer saw it was Peter Bullock and he had been washing his hands in the basin put there for the purpose of cleaning sacred vessels.

Bullock was one of the two town constables, paid by the merchant guilds to maintain a semblance of law. He acted as proxy for rich traders too busy to shoulder their own responsibilities. He was a squat man with a bent back and a permanent scowl for a face. Still, he bore his infirmity well and his patience in his dealings with the more powerful proctors of the university had appealed to Falconer when he first met him: an occasion when one of his students had unwisely assumed he could get away with cheating a baker of the few coins required to purchase some bread. The student had been drunk, the baker unwilling to let the matter drop even after Falconer had paid him what was owed. A constable had been called and Bullock had taken the baker aside and turned his anger into a grudging acceptance of the coins and a few pence more in compensation. Afterwards

Falconer had asked the constable what had changed the baker's mind. He had laughed and said he had merely reminded the baker that he might no longer be able to turn a blind eye to the certain overcharging of some customers. Falconer's academic mind had been pleased by this practical application of logic, and a relationship had developed between two men of quite different stations in life.

Bullock's heavy figure seemed carved out of stone – as though he were part of the cross beside which he now stood. He looked to Falconer like a sad God musing at the figures of Adam and Eve eating from the tree of knowledge, his breath visible in cold blasts that chilled humanity. Falconer turned to the form on the heavy oak table in the middle of the chapel. The girl had clearly been quite attractive in life, and some effort had been made to remove the obvious signs of the attack. Someone had cleaned the blood from her face, and it was now framed by a fringe of wet hair that clung to her cheeks, no longer housing the bloom of youth as they must have done only hours before. However, lurid splashes of dark red stained the front of her plain grey shift and the slash across her throat still gaped like an awful second mouth.

'Who is . . . was she?' asked Falconer as he crossed to the table to examine the body more closely.

'Only a servant.'

Bullock's voice seemed strained and harsh, carrying an ironic note that Falconer had not noticed before. He looked up and Bullock sighed.

'Margaret Gebetz, a French girl employed by Master Fyssh.'

'Fyssh? Of Beke's Inn? Was that him I passed in the lane?'

'The same. He has already been here to identify her. You would know better than I, but no doubt he brought her back from his time in Paris.'

32

'Do you suspect him of the killing?'

Bullock hesitated, knowing Falconer's own interest in suspicious deaths.

'Maybe. Which puts it out of my hands.'

Falconer ignored the reference to the university's jealously guarded right to deal with its own and peered closely at the wound, then lifted both arms and looked at them. The girl's hands were cold to his touch and though their owner could no longer feel anything, he was moved enough to gently lay them back, linked across the body.

'You've cleaned the hands, too,' he said, straightening the wet hair around her face.

'No. I only wiped the face.'

Falconer paused, then nodded.

'Of course. I've seen all I want to see,' he said and made to go through the arch past Bullock.

The constable grasped his arm with a firm hand and spoke quietly into his ear.

'I cannot be responsible for what may happen today. Certain people in the town need only the slightest excuse to show the university what they think of it.'

He waved at the still form on the table, which in the gathering gloom of the storm-filled sky took on the appearance of a carved effigy on a tomb, stiff and lifeless.

'This is more than they need.'

Chapter Three

The streets of Oxford at this hour would normally be waking to the noise of students, refreshed by a simple draught of ale and a stale crust from the day before. Like streamlets pouring into one great confluence, bodies garbed in a rich variety of styles and colours would rouse any late risers with their robust chatter as they filled every narrow lane leading to the High Street. Richer clerks, destined for high office of State, favoured brighter colours – scarlet and blue – whereas the tunics of poorer ones were confined to rustic browns. Scattered in the crowd would be the more sober attire of the Masters, crowned with fur-lined hoods. All would be making their way to Schools Street, that narrow lane of rooms hired by the Masters to teach in their different faculties.

Also at this time the traders of the town would be lowering their wooden shutters to form counters to display their wares. The smell of bakers at their work would cause many a hungry student to yearn for his dinner, four hours away between terce and sext. The sight of sides of meat at the butcher's would cause the student entrusted with the purchase of food for his hall to think what his farthing might fetch him. The smell of ale and wine mingled with that of leather in the bootmaker's. Outnumbering the students as they did, the ordinary people of the town lived in an uneasy truce with the university. Successive royal charters had asserted the power of the chancellor over the town. Still, there was a living to be made out of so many hungry mouths, even if the chancellor regulated the traders' profits. What did they care if St Augustine had proclaimed business an evil that turned men from true rest in God? Didn't a man have to live and feed his family?

This morning that truce seemed to be on the verge of being broken, and the streets of Oxford were unusually quiet. A few foolhardy students, calling loudly to each other with nervous bravado, passed the window arch of the main room in Aristotle's hall. The chill wind carried their voices in to Thomas, who shuddered and turned back to Hugh Pett. He had missed what Hugh was telling him in his desire to get out and explore Oxford.

'Sorry, what did you say?'

'I was saying as you've already mastered grammar, Master Falconer may progress you straight to the rest of the trivium.' His pale face was turned solemnly at the younger boy. *'Inter artes quae dicuntur trivium, fundatrix Grammatica vendicat principium.'*

Thomas looked glumly at his feet and scuffed the bare clay ground of the hall. He felt Hugh's arm around his, then a playful punch to his side. The other boy was grinning.

'Don't worry. There are plenty of boys whose Latin is terrible. In the early days all you are required to do is sit and listen, then follow the repetitions.'

Hugh passed him a book that he had been holding in his hand since showing Thomas where he was to sleep – a room shared with two other clerks. The room was dark, even well into the morning, its one unglazed window looked out on the wall of the building across the narrow lane. It was impossible to tell much about the room aside from the fact that it housed three stark wooden beds and a single chair. Living in the country as he had, Thomas was unused to the constrictions of the cheek-by-jowl houses in Oxford.

In contrast to his room, Hugh's was neat and boasted a view which revealed the walls of the city looming over the rooftops opposite. Hugh had taken the book he was now giving Thomas from a small collection on a shelf above his bed, itself covered by a patterned quilt. At the foot of the bed stood a carved chest, suggesting that Hugh Pett had even more rich clothes.

'Take this, and study it. I must go and prepare for my Responsions. Remember what the Master said about not leaving the hall.'

Thomas sighed and turned his attention to the battered text in his hands.

Master Fyssh had bullied one of his students in Beke's Inn into providing a crust of bread and some cheese, and another had some ale left over from the previous night's drinking. No one, least of all Fyssh, relished the thought of being abroad in Oxford when the town was looking for a murderer. Especially if he himself were suspected. He had to make do with these leftovers until tempers quietened down. Now he sat at the table in the common hall picking the crumbs of bread from his sizeable stomach, cursing the girl as though she had deliberately died to ruin his digestion. The tankard at his elbow was empty and his students kept to their rooms in fear of Fyssh's ill mood.

He knew he should be lecturing, but who but the most foolish student would expect him? He cupped his many chins in his hands and stared disconsolately into the empty mug. A hard hand descending on to his shoulder caused him to shriek and knock the mug flying. The last dregs of ale stained his lavish gown, and he turned to be confronted by an ugly pock-marked face well known to him.

'Moulcom!'

Jack Moulcom's pitted face split in a grimace hardly recognizable as a smile. His black hair was plastered greasily across his forehead and his eyes were like small pieces of coal set in a sea of pockmarks. His surcoat belied the coarseness of that face; it was red and of a rich material, yet somehow graceless on the clerk's frame. For he was only a clerk, yet still Fyssh feared him. He sat on the bench staring up with his jaw hanging open and his chins wobbling. Moulcom set a hard hand on each of Fyssh's shoulders and stared into his eyes.

'The girl's room.' His accent was harsh and of the North.

'Wh-what?'

'The girl's room. Where is it?' The hands clenched harder on Fyssh's shoulders, squeezing the statement from him.

'Through there.' He turned his terrified look to the end door of the hall where Margaret Gebetz had had her quarters. Moulcom gave one final squeeze, strode to the door and flung it open. After he had disappeared Fyssh called out in his piping voice.

'Damn you, you can't treat a regent master in this way. The Northern Proctor shall hear of it.'

His voice tailed off along with his short-lived bravado as the oddly dressed student returned to the hall.

'I think not. Not if you don't want them to be told what I know of you and your little habits.'

His eyes pierced Fyssh who seemed to deflate and collapse back on to the bench, an empty bag. Turning back to the door, he flung a warning over his shoulder.

'You wait there, and if any of your students come, get rid of them.'

Fyssh sat still, his body shaking with terror. He nervously drew his fat forefinger through the puddle of ale on the table top and absently sucked it. A crash of furniture in the other room made him wince. It was followed by the sound of pots echoing as they bounced on the floor. Fyssh pressed his hands to his ears, trying to shut out the sound of Moulcom becoming more and more angry. If he couldn't find what he wanted, what would he do to the regent master? And what could he possibly want from amongst the paltry possessions of a dead servant girl?

Falconer stood at the entrance to St Frideswide's deep in thought. Should he once again get involved in a mystery – for this was no straightforward killing, he was sure of that – or should he keep to the promise he made the chancellor after the Godstow affair? He sighed, why was he fooling himself that he had a choice? He could not relax until he had solved this particular problem. Especially as the townspeople seemed, according to Bullock, so incensed by the slaying. As he went to turn back to Aristotle's hall, a voice called him from the opposite direction.

'Falconer. I want to talk to you.'

William sighed again – it was the voice of de Stepyng whose instruction in the law Schools seemed to him to be fastidious to the extent of dullness. He had obviously come from there for Falconer's hazy vision could discern his shape coming out of the end of Vine Hall Lane. As he approached, Falconer's judgement as to the ownership of the voice was confirmed. Robert de Stepyng was as fastidious in his appearance as his mind. His plain black gown with white trimmed hood was topped by a sallow face with a hawk-like nose. His close cropped hair emphasized the sharpness of his features, even his ears appeared pointed at the top.

'I understand that someone has died.'

'Murdered. That is so.' Falconer thought how strange it was

that everyone slipped into de Stepyng's clipped speech in his presence.

'That should still not prevent the students from attending their normal lectures at the set hour.'

Falconer felt a gust of chill wind along the lane and looked up to the sky. It was clouding over and threatening to rain.

'Bullock thinks the townsmen are ready to riot, so perhaps it is sensible of the students to stay indoors. I have told mine to do so.'

'Bullock?' De Stepyng's question came of the impatience of someone who wished everything defined.

'One of the town constables.'

'Oh.' He clearly thought that definition left the man in question not worthy of any further consideration. 'A town girl killed by her own kind, no doubt. They would cut each other's throats for a stale loaf. Not known to me and therefore no concern of mine. Or yours, Falconer.'

De Stepyng too was clearly recalling William's previous involvements. Falconer shuddered as another driving gust of wind blew and spots of rain began to fall. As he drew his gown around him, he noticed that the weather seemed not to affect the calm of the other man. It was as if even the wind was afraid to disturb his precision.

De Stepyng turned and went towards St Aldate's without another word, a dark figure disappearing into the gloom of gathering clouds, leaving Falconer with a niggling thought that he could not pin down.

Thomas was tired of sitting in the cold hall at Aristotle's. He had come to Oxford expecting something more than boredom, and the fright of the previous night had receded. Hugh and the other students were keeping to their rooms, and Thomas did

39

not feel like disturbing the people he was to share with just yet. He looked idly through the window arch then leaned right out. The street was dead quiet both ways and Thomas could not see that it would be dangerous to be abroad. He would just explore the immediate area – Hugh had said the houses the other side of Shidyerd Street belonged to Jews. He had heard many tales about Jews but had never seen one. His father had once told him of a Jew called Samuel who lived in Bristol. He had enticed a boy called Adam into his house and crucified him with his wife's connivance. His father had not spared any gory details and Thomas shuddered to recollect it. The story went on to tell how a voice from God had shamed the wife into confession. She had resolved to accept Christian baptism, but Samuel had killed her in anger. Thus his father warned him of the outcast Jews and their evilness, though he had not seen one himself.

Of course Thomas did not believe the story, even if the Jews had crucified our Lord. Still, it would be interesting to satisfy his curiosity about this cursed race who lived by lending money. Thomas slipped the book by Donatus inside his jerkin and quietly opened the main door to the hall. There was no one around and although the sky looked dark, he decided it was safe enough and turned right down towards the Jewish quarter.

Although the cellar was icy cold and the rain outside slanted through the narrow arch close to the ceiling, the body was putrefying. He would have to bury it tonight before his neighbours started complaining of the stench. It did not seem to affect him, he accepted the smell as a simple necessity. Almost a pleasure, as its connotation was the exercise of his skill with a knife. He scooped together the detritus of his carving, casting entrails, bones and muscle into a bloody jumble in the sack.

His work was unfinished and this sample had not revealed all that he would wish. What a pity the servant girl was steadfastly guarded by that ugly toad of a man. For what Bonham truly needed was a fresh human body.

Chapter Four

The freezing rain began to tumble out of the darkening sky and urged Falconer into some form of action. He could not stand outside St Frideswide's any longer trying to make the few scraps of information available to him expand into a logical whole. Beke's Inn was to hand and so now perhaps was the time to talk to Master Fyssh. He turned to his right and hurried down the lane, which was already turning to mud in the torrent of water falling from the sky. Squeezing into the shallow doorway of Beke's Inn, he plastered his soaked hair flat on his head and knocked. After a pause he heard a shuffling behind the door but it did not open. He knocked again, more impatiently as water ran down the back of his neck.

'Who is it?' the voice piped tremulously, barely audible through the thick oak door.

'Fyssh. Open up, it's Falconer of Aristotle's.'

'What do you want?'

'At the moment I would like to be somewhere warm and dry. Open up for heaven's sake.'

The voice behind the door made a grumbling noise, then Falconer heard the grating of rarely used bolts. One piggy eye set deep in a fat face applied itself to the crack as the door barely opened. Falconer impatiently set his fist against the oak and pushed the startled Fyssh aside as though he were no weight at all. He squealed like a pig and cowered in the corner holding on to the edge of the door as if it were a shield.

'There's no need to be afraid. I am alone.'

He prised Fyssh's fingers off the door and closed it behind him, shutting out the hiss of the rain. Fyssh's jowls quivered, a tear trickling down his fat cheek. As Falconer looked at the other man, he cursed his own abruptness. He had obviously been so scared today already that he was near to collapse. It would not help the cause of uncovering a few facts if Falconer had a fit of hysterics to contend with. He gently extended his arm, and with it around Fyssh's shoulder guided the shaken man to a bench near the hearth. He placed himself squarely before the fire and his wet clothes steamed.

'That's a relief. It's like the time of Noah's flood out there.'

He let the other man compose himself, taking the opportunity to look around the hall. It appeared almost opulent in comparison with his own bare accommodation – there was even a tapestry hung on one wall. It was said Fyssh taught few students and yet he obviously did not lack money. He even had a servant girl – or did until last night. It was Fyssh himself who broke the silence.

'I suppose you too wish to question me about that damned girl.'

'Too?'

'Yes. That surly hunchback dragged me to see the body, practically accusing me of murder with his looks. And then . . .'

Fyssh hesitated, his eyes dropping to the floor just as Falconer thought he had recovered his usual bluster. Something had scared him; was it fear of discovery? Falconer sat in silence, but the man had clearly decided to say no more. He sat looking at the fire, nervously stroking the fur on the cuff of his loose-fitting gown. It was obvious to Falconer he would have to press him despite his delicate mental condition. He began indirectly.

'What was Margaret doing abroad so late last night?'

'What?' Fyssh's eyes suddenly focused on his questioner. 'That I do not know.'

'When did you last see her?'

Fyssh explained that she had served his dinner at nones and provided for the students in the hall. After she cleared his bowls, he neither knew nor cared what she was about. She had a bed in the kitchen. Falconer suspected Fyssh knew nothing because he had been drunk. But on the other hand could he in that state have caused the girl's death?

'And her possessions?'

'What do I care of her possessions? If indeed she had any.' Fyssh was becoming increasingly peevish. 'She was a servant.'

It was clear he thought this sufficient to know about her. Falconer came to the crucial question.

'And you? Where were you when she died?'

Strangely this did not seem to anger Fyssh. Indeed, his response was quite considered as though he were innocent of her murder. Or perhaps had prepared himself well.

'I fell asleep soon after dinner. I do not recall anything else until I was woken by that constable this morning. Indeed I do not know when she was killed precisely.'

Falconer sighed and asked if he could see where she slept. Fyssh's eyes flickered towards the kitchen door and his face paled. Unsure what this reaction betokened, Falconer made to move towards the kitchen. The fat man's reaction was swift and unexpected.

'No you may not.'

He lurched from his seat, his jowls quivering and his face turning pale. Spittle flew from his lips as he cursed Falconer and his rage gave him enough courage to grasp his arm and urge him towards the door. Surprised and amused at this strange show of bravado, Falconer allowed himself to be deposited out in the lane. Clearly he was to get no further with Fyssh; at least for the present. But what had he said to cause the reaction?

The other side of the door, Fyssh felt safe as he pushed the bolts home. He rested his flabby cheek against the smooth oak and breathed out in relief. Moulcom's coarse voice close to his ear caused him to stiffen again with shock. He had not heard the young man creep up behind him.

'You did well to get rid of him. Now let us talk about the matter of the girl's book.'

'I know of no book. She was a servant; what would she be doing with a book?'

Fyssh winced as Moulcom raised a rough red fist over his head and grasped the fur around his collar with the other. His breath reeked of ale as he thrust his face at Fyssh, twisting the cloth in his grasp so that it cut into the Master's neck.

'She had no book or papers?'

'No, I swear,' he croaked. Moulcom twisted until the cloth cut deep into the blotchy red flesh and Fyssh's face turned purple, his eyes bulging with real fear.

'If I find you are lying . . .' His threat hung in the air between them. Then he threw the choking Fyssh to the floor and left, leaving the Master to wonder about the importance of the dead girl's book.

Falconer, standing in a doorway next to Beke's Inn, watched the ugly form of the student disappear down the lane towards Fish Street. Despite the handicap of his eyes, and the student's form being huddled against the rain, he recognized him as Jack Moulcom from the Northern Nation who had already earned a bad reputation amongst other students. Why had Fyssh gone to such pains to conceal the fact that he was present just now? A flash of lightning and a momentous clap of thunder urged

Falconer to get indoors before he was as drowned as all those animals who failed to enter the Ark.

Thomas's heart nearly stopped at the clap of thunder. He wished he had not left the security of Aristotle's, for he now stood in an alley in the Jewry – he was convinced by the heap of rubbish at his feet. He could not be sure, but the broken pot with two feet pointing to the sky like the Devil's horns seemed to mock his sense of direction. All the alleys and blind doors seemed the same. And every shuttered window turned its back on him as the rain beat down. Fear of becoming another murdered Hugh of Lincoln prevented him from beating on a door at random and seeking either shelter or directions. The stories his father had told now seemed not so far-fetched.

Indeed he thought he heard the baying of the Devil's hound already. He could discern sharp barking notes ringing down the alleys, and imagined the sharp-toothed creatures making them. Then he realized it was the sound of human voices and they were coming his way. The heart that had nearly stopped now beat with the speed of some demented blacksmith. For the second time in two days he was being hunted. Was life in towns always like this? He began to yearn for the boredom of his father's farm. He tried to work out where the sound of the mob was coming from so that he might retreat in the opposite direction. At least a choice of direction would now be forced upon him. Splashing through the clinging mud, he ran to one end of the narrow alley which split into two. Trying to still the thudding of his heart, he listened and groaned. The angry voices echoed up both alleys. His only option was to retreat the way he had come and that had resulted in his losing his way.

He leaned both his hands on the rough wood of a door to

gain his breath, and stumbled forward as it gave in to his weight. He regained his footing and looked up, fearing the worst. But he stood alone in a gloomy hall – he had been let in by the merest chance of a bolt that had been carelessly thrown.

He turned to go back out through the door, which still hung ajar, but the sound of harsh voices, already in the alley baying to each other, changed his mind. He slammed the door and threw the bolt firmly in place this time. Turning, he leaned his back against the door feeling the safety of its solidness, only to open his eyes to a more terrifying sight.

Falconer had hardly reached the doorway of Aristotle's when he heard the clamour of a church bell. The sound was distant and tinny – it was the bell of St Martin's, clearly a rallying call for the townspeople. He stood in the arch of the door and listened. Shortly the sound of ox-horns blared out and Falconer knew the hue and cry was up and could not be stopped. Foolish students would probably respond and call others to battle with them. Wise foxes like Falconer went to earth until the madness was over. The townspeople, as Bullock had warned, were incensed by the death of one of their own and were too ready to blame their old enemy, the university. There would be no recourse to common sense and reasoning, merely a foolishness which both sides would have to repent later. Falconer slammed the door of Aristotle's behind him and sighed.

'Falconer, is that you?'

He screwed his eyes up to focus better on the figure standing at the end of the dark passage leading to the hall. Even though it was still afternoon – scarcely nones – the dullness of the day did little more than make the man a grey shape to Falconer. It was still too early for the extravagance of lighting candles, and

William silently cursed his weak sight. He played for time, not wishing anyone to know of his failing, and walked towards the man.

'Who else would it be, entering Aristotle's as if he owned its walls? Though you seem to have made yourself at home here, Bonham,' he growled, at last recognizing the man before him.

Richard Bonham was a nondescript regent master of rhetoric, very fond of quoting St Augustine on the evils of trade. Bonham was a small man, in thinking and in stature, with a bald head that resembled a Franciscan tonsure. Indeed his clothes were simple and often a dull grey, so that he could have been taken for a friar.

He disregarded Falconer's pointed comment, and began to ask him about his friendship with Peter Bullock. His purpose soon became obvious. Unlike de Stepying, he was very interested in the dead girl.

'I was wondering if, through your intercession, I might be allowed to dispose of the body suitably.'

Responding to the query in Falconer's eyes, he went on quickly.

'After all, she has no family and I would like to ensure she has a Christian burial.' He took the other man's arm as if to hasten his decision. But there was simply no contest between his puny frame and the solid bulk of Falconer. The latter simply stood his ground, stopping Bonham in his tracks.

'I think not. At least not at the moment – the hunt is up out there and you may be foolhardy enough to brave it, but not I.'

The little man seemed about to retort, but he held his counsel and stepped to the narrow slit of a window that overlooked the lane. He cocked his thin face to one side and listened. He reminded Falconer of a cautious songthrush spying out the land with one eye while keeping both ears open for warning noises. The hoarse cry of townspeople echoed in the distance, and Bonham's lips pursed even tighter as though more annoyed that the other man was right.

'In that case, as I appear to be forced to stay here, may I take the opportunity to correct your errors recently enunciated to the poor clerks who depend on your teaching for their progress through the quadrivium?'

Falconer breathed a heavy sigh – Bonham was a pedantic thinker with whom discussion could be long and tedious.

'Which errors might they be?'

'I understand that you continue to insist that the world is shaped like a cape.' A condescending smile split the small man's face, the corners of his mouth turned down registering disapproval. 'And though I do not subscribe to the theory of Cosmas in his work *Topographia Christiana* that the world is shaped as is the tabernacle of God, surely Isidore's view sums up the accurate Christian position.'

His eyes fixed Falconer, daring him to contradict. But the other man knew better and Bonham continued.

'A T within an O succinctly describes the division of the world amongst the sons of Noah. Shem was granted Asia, a full half of the world in accordance with the concept of primogeniture. Europe was the portion of Japheth—'

The diatribe was interrupted by the crashing open of the heavy oak door. An unusually dishevelled Hugh Pett flew through only to be stopped in his tracks by the sight of a disapproving Richard Bonham.

'Master!'

Pett's eyes held a wild appeal, but Bonham raised his hand and prevented further words from the young student. The regent master patiently continued. 'Europe was the portion of Japheth, and Africa that of Ham.'

'The cape you so ridicule is merely the attempt of the ancient Ptolemy to depict on a flat surface the curvature of the world.'

Pett could contain himself no longer. 'Master, I must speak to you.'

This time it was Falconer's turn to raise his hand. Bonham's smugness had angered him and he was determined to beat him with logical argument.

'Quiet, Hugh.' He turned his gaze to the regent master, who sat primly on the bench safe in his own certitude.

'Do you deny the world is curved? I myself have sat atop a mast at sea and spied land before someone on the deck of the ship. Even your elementary knowledge of geometry will permit you to see the significance of that – a demonstrable fact.'

'Master, Thomas is missing,' Hugh blurted out before he could be stopped again. 'I think he went out and he's not returned.'

Falconer reacted immediately, leaping from his chair and knocking an ale jug into the lap of the startled Bonham. He grasped the silk collar of Pett's gown and thrust him down next to the older man.

'Tell me, where could he have gone?'

Hugh hesitated.

'Come, he must have said something about wanting to see things for himself. If not, you must remember what it was like coming here for the first time. What were you most curious about? Think!'

Hugh frowned in concentration as he tried to recall the flood of questions Thomas had plied him with that morning. Something struck him.

'He made some silly comment about ritual murder. Of course I did not believe him—'

'Jewry.' Falconer danced towards the door, calling over his shoulder.

'Both of you stay here. No. Hugh – first bolt the street door behind me, then wait for my return. Don't leave under any circumstances.'

He was through the door before Hugh Pett was on his feet. Yet hardly had he begun to hurry after his Master to throw the bolt than Falconer came back and wagged a finger at him.

'And if anything has happened to that boy . . .'

The threat was left unfinished, but Pett blanched knowing that the boy had been his charge. He began to speak, but Falconer was already gone.

Chapter Five

T he terrifying form occupied the hallway before Thomas, black and massive. His hair was a wild tangle in which Thomas was sure he could discern horns. Steam issued from between his hands and the boy was certain he could smell the charnel odour of hell. He cringed in the doorway and made the sign of the cross. Undeterred the figure came towards him, the steam swirling around his dark robes. Rooted to the spot, Thomas could only look up in horror, thinking of all the children who had been human sacrifices on the altar of the Jews. The eyes of the monster glowed redly in the dark corridor, transfixing him. He thought he heard the cry of someone behind his tormentor, calling in some outlandish language. It could only be the Jew's familiar − a cat or a goat, his father had once assured him. Thomas fell to his knees and prepared himself for death.

Falconer heard Hugh slam the bolts behind him and slipped down the alley, dodging from door to door. At least the rain had stopped for the moment, though the afternoon was still miserable. The cries of people and the clash of arms came mainly from the direction of the High Street. Falconer kept to the lanes near the city walls. The boy had spoken about ritual murder, the current nonsense laid at the doorstep of the Jews. Perhaps he was now exhibiting a farmboy's curiosity to see this persecuted race, and had made for Jewry. Anyway, this was

Falconer's only clue to his possible whereabouts. He prayed that he was right and the boy had the sense to keep away from the main confrontation. Crossing Shidyerd Street, Falconer's feet squelched through the mud on the spot where the girl had been killed. He thought again of the truths he had collected about the death, so terribly few to date, and was frustrated that no deductive truth resulted from them. He collided with a man coming round the corner as though chased by the Devil. His ale-laden breath assaulted Falconer as the man clung to his clothes, his eyes staring wildly into the Master's.

Falconer squared his shoulders to beat off an attack but the man could only muster a curse before he loosened his grasp and staggered down the lane. He cast a glance over his shoulder and was gone. Falconer breathed a sigh of relief and turned up the narrow alley that led deep into Jewry. The grim buildings crowded in on him, dripping rainwater from their eaves into the churned mud of the lanes. At least they afforded some safety from the riot which carried over to Falconer as muffled cries ebbing to and fro away to his right. The time for harassing the Jews was not now – the town had other fish to fry. The only risk was turning down Vine Hall Lane, when he would be momentarily visible from the High Street. His poor eyesight meant he would not know if anyone was looking down the lane as he emerged and crossed to the other side. He decided he would have to risk it. Having come this far, he was determined to ensure the safety of Thomas if he could.

Thomas de Cantilupe was concerned for his own safety. As chancellor he had much to lose besides his dignity. But even his life would be worth nothing, if he could not control the university and its constant squabbles with the town. The King might be on the verge of plunging the country into all-out civil war, but he could still be petitioned to penalize the university for any perceived wrong. And he was unhappy with the student body, who seemed to be siding with Earl Simon. If de Cantilupe could not walk the tightrope of diplomacy, his ambitions, which stretched far beyond Oxford, would be thwarted.

He had only just concluded a meeting with the new proctor elected by the Masters of the North, when the clanging of St Martin's church bell caused the hairs on his neck to prickle. He had sent away the proctor to exercise some control over his students, and hurried into the street still clad in his formal academical cope. Its heavy purple folds swirled about him as he bustled down the High Street, hoping to divert any foolhardy members of his university from being dragged into a fight. Besides he now needed urgently to see Jack Moulcom.

He cursed upon seeing two foolish students swaggering down the road in front of him, one brandishing a sword. The rain beat down on them, soaking their clothes, but they seemed oblivious to it. The one with the sword placed his feet wide apart in the clinging mud and swung his weapon in a great arc, his back to the chancellor. His companion looked on admiringly as the braggart roared with all his might for an adversary. They giggled together as there came no response save the growl of thunder in the air. De Cantilupe strode up behind them unobserved and, as the swordsman wound himself up for another display, he spoke.

'Fools, do you want to die so young?'

His quiet but firm voice stopped both young men in their tracks. As the one with the sword swivelled round to see who was commanding him, his sword plunged at de Cantilupe's feet. Fortunately the heavy folds of his cope diverted the blade, but a long tear appeared in the sumptuous gown. De Cantilupe looked down, and the student blanched realizing whose robe he had just ruined. His nerveless fingers loosened on the sword, and de Cantilupe took it from his grasp. He sighed, surveying the damage to the cope, already soaking up the noxious stew of fluids coursing down the centre of the road.

'I believe this weapon will be safer with me. And you will be safer within the walls of your hall. Go there. Immediately.'

The students looked crestfallen and, stumbling over an apology, backed away from the chancellor. He watched them go towards a side lane leading to Jewry, then spotted a mob at the far end of the High Street coming his way. With a sword in his hand, his life would be as at risk as the students' would have been, and he did not think his cope would save him from harm again. He turned back to the safety of his hall, hoping the students would not be seen by the town mob. His business with Moulcom would just have to wait.

Falconer paused at the mouth of the alley, leaning against the timber of a corner building. Cursing his poor vision, he squinted to his right. As he did so, two figures were outlined at the junction of the lane with the High Street. They appeared to be arguing momentarily, one clutching the other's sleeve. A distant cry seemed to resolve their disagreement, and they turned towards Falconer. However, they had hardly gone a few yards, when a half a dozen shapes darkened the entrance to the lane. Two students, incautiously or with foolish bravado, had clearly ventured out of doors. Now they had been spotted by the mob and were no match for them. Falconer prayed that Thomas was not one of them.

Turning to look over his shoulder, one of the pursued slipped in the mud, bringing his fellow down with him. In a moment the pursuing gang were on them and rained blows with their clubs on their defenceless victims. Falconer heard the sickening crunch of broken bones and was roused from the daze caused by the suddenness of the incident. Without thinking, he sprang from his hiding place and bore down on the thugs screaming at the top of his voice.

It may be that his sudden and seemingly mad appearance saved him from the fate of the two boys. The ranks of the gang wavered and broke, and they fled away in the direction they had come from. It may be that their own insane urge to kill had been broken by the very act of killing. They were, after all, just ordinary townspeople in other circumstances. The two students lay on their backs, their blood mingled in one pool. Their faces were cruelly lacerated but Falconer could tell that neither was Thomas. It was equally clear that both were dead.

With nothing to be done for them, Falconer's main concern was still Thomas and his only hope was to contact Rabbi Jehoza-dok at the Scola Judaeorum. If Thomas was alive and hiding somewhere in Jewry, the Rabbi would know, or be able to find out where he was. A Jew's life in England hung in a precarious balance and depended on alertness to those surrounding them.

Jews were the King's property, and could only exist in England to do him service. That service was to be milked for money by the spendthrift Henry, who only a few years ago had mortgaged them like some unwanted derelict house to his brother, Richard of Cornwall. They were grudgingly respected by the merchants who had dealings with them, and hated by de Montfort and the barons. The latter had sworn to destroy the *archa* kept by the Jews – a registry of bonds in each major trading centre. This de Montfort especially desired as he himself had borrowed the princely sum of one hundred and ten pounds from them.

Many people feared and hated the Jews, but Falconer's own prejudice had been overcome as a youth far from England, and was based on an admiration of the scholarship of the people. Indeed it had been the old Rabbi Jehozadok himself who had allowed Falconer to borrow rare copies of the two great books of the Arab, Avicenna – the *Qanun* and the *Shifa*. The last Falconer greatly prized for its interpretation of Aristotle's ideas.

Another flurry of rain washed the blood off the clerks' brutalized faces and, with a sigh, Falconer turned away to seek out his old friend the rabbi. He was soon at the doors of the Scola and had no need to knock before the heavy oak was swung open briefly to let him in. He stood brushing the rain from his eyes and the reassuring voice of the old rabbi came from behind him.

'You are taking a very great chance, my friend. It must be important, what you seek.'

Jehozadok's voice was deep and firm, belying his years. His gnarled hands, bent with age, fumbled on the bolts of the door and Falconer helped him secure the synagogue. A woven shawl was wrapped around the Jew's shoulders and thick white locks tumbled from his head, mingling with his beard, their meeting point almost indistinguishable. His dark features were heavily lined and, although his eyes bore the faded cast of age, they clearly betokened the sharpness of the man's mind. He looked hard into Falconer's own troubled eyes.

'Come with me. You are in need of something to soothe that fearsome look.'

He took Falconer by the arm and led him down a dark corridor to its end and lifted a heavy curtain. The room beyond glowed in candlelight, revealing a wall lined with books. Even Falconer, a lover of strange texts and used to the accumulated wealth of books in the hands of the university, was always excited by this library. A large tome lay open on the oaken table beneath the candelabra.

'I am afraid my eyes cannot cope with most of these texts now. I read them mostly from memory rather than the page.'

Falconer sat at the table, while the rabbi fussed with a pitcher of wine. The book was in a language unknown to him and he was curious to enquire what it was. But the possible fate of Thomas was more urgent and he dragged his eyes from the page to explain his errand. Between draughts of the sweet red wine that had been proffered him, he asked if Jehozadok could enquire of his people if a student new to the town had been seen or taken in. The old man called out in his own language, and a young man with a wispy beard lifted the curtain. He must have been standing just behind it so sudden was his appearance. Jehozadok spoke to him, and he disappeared as silently as he had come.

'Joshua will find your student, if he is to be found.' The old man's voice was reassuring. 'Now tell me what your opinion is of the text by Avicenna that I gave you.'

Jack Moulcom had delayed returning to his employer, knowing he would not be happy at his not finding the book. Still, what could he expect if he did not explain what the book was, merely that it would be obvious when he saw it? He had not seen it and that was that. The rainstorm and the early clashes of townspeople and students, warning of the battle that had now arrived, drove him indoors to face the older man. His greatest fears had been realized. The man's face was dark with rage; even in the gloom of the ill-lit room that much was clear to Moulcom.

'Fool, I cannot trust you to do anything. You even alerted Fyssh to what you were looking for. That could be dangerous.'

Moulcom scratched his greasy locks and mumbled in his rough Northern tones, 'There was nothing to find.'

'I was stupid to think you could even identify a book if you saw one. When was the last time you attended a lesson?'

Moulcom's incoherent excuses were brushed aside by a curt wave of the older man's hand. He paced the dark and claustro-phobic room, and Moulcom dared not move.

'If only the girl had not died.'

The man was clearly angry at the poor girl's presump-tuousness.

Moulcom sat in the corner racking his brain for a ploy to please this harsh taskmaster. The man was muttering to himself in a language unknown to the puzzled student. Remembering the interruption to his search, Moulcom mentioned Fyssh's unexpected visitor.

'Master Falconer came while I was searching.'

The pacing stopped abruptly.

'He saw you?'

Moulcom explained that he had hidden in the back room and threatened Fyssh with death if he didn't get rid of the visitor. He assured the other man that Falconer had left none the wiser. Indeed he might already suspect Fyssh of the murder.

'And perhaps it was Fyssh. She was his servant – maybe she did not wash the dishes to his satisfaction.'

Moulcom forced a weak laugh at his master's witticism. A cruel smile was returned by the man.

'I merely want the return of something which is precious to me. And being dead, the girl will find it difficult to do so herself.'

The man's response led Moulcom to think some good humour had been restored. And he could no longer restrain his curiosity.

'Would this book link the girl to you?'

When no reply came, his coarse mind made the only connection he was capable of, and with a giggle he spoke the words, 'They all said she went with men. Did you have her?'

Even his employer's piercing eyes turned on him could not stay his tumbling tongue.

'Was she good?'

'That's enough, blasphemer.'

Moulcom could not believe the power of the man's hands on his throat. He would have wagered on his own physical strength against this book man. He clasped the other's wrists but could not move them.

'God save me,' he croaked, with what air he had left.

'God will not save you.'

The man's eyes bore triumphantly into Moulcom's.

'The Devil created you and all you see around you. How could the good God be responsible for anything but pure spirit. That's why there will be no Resurrection such as you fools are taught. So look your last on the physical world.'

Moulcom was filled with horror. He cared not a jot for heresy, even if he had been able to identify it as such. The horror was in the power of the words and that of the hands around his throat. His fists beat a weakening tattoo on the other's back to no avail.

'But, fear not. Your soul will survive to be cast over the precipice by demons.'

The man's face pressed up against his, but Moulcom could read nothing more in his eyes. He just felt weary and fearful for what was to come. What had he said to deserve this? He still did not understand as those cold eyes faded into a grey mist of oblivion. He would have sworn the last sound he heard was the jingle of horse armour.

*   *   *

Try as he could, Falconer was not able to concentrate on Jehoza-dok's exposition of the difference between the Two Wisdoms. He could only think of his own lack of wisdom in leaving Thomas to his own devices. Was he now dead, when only so recently arrived in Oxford? The rabbi's gentle chiding brought his thoughts back to the moment.

'I can see my teaching on Sophia and Phronesis have not served to distract you from the boy and his fate.'

'Forgive me, Rabbi. I—'

Falconer's need to put his feelings into words was obviated by the return of the young Jew. He glided silently over to Jehozadok, and leaned over him with his back to Falconer, rainwater dripping from his sodden clothes. He whispered something in the older man's ear that Falconer could not catch and then turned his impassive gaze on the gentile. His cold eyes betrayed a dislike for Falconer but nothing of the import of his message. The Oxford Master's gaze turned anxiously on the elderly Jew, anticipating the worst. The rabbi's face broke into a smile.

'Good news, my friend. The boy is safe. He is in the home of Samson the herbalist. Joshua here will conduct you safely to him.'

Though he was hungry and the food before him was tempting, Thomas could not drag his eyes from the beautiful face of the Jewish girl. Her own eyes were brown and large, her red lips contrasted with her ivory skin. He stared at them as they moved, not taking in the words she was saying. She laughed and teased him.

'You obviously think it not important to listen to the words of a mere girl, brave scholar.'

Thomas flushed red and stammered an apology. He did not

want to offend Hannah. After all, this was the first girl of any beauty that he had encountered. In his village his only knowledge was of red-faced wenches who claimed a greater sexual experience than he. Indeed they ignored him as a mere youth. Now he had met a girl who was prepared to talk to him as a man, and he did not know what to say. He cursed his inexperience.

Coming round from his faint earlier, his first sight had been of her face and he could have imagined himself in Heaven. Fortunately he had had no opportunity to embarrass himself further by saying anything. The demon who had caused his faint had appeared over the shoulder of the girl. But in the full light of several candles it was clear he was only an old man, with a concerned expression on his face. Admittedly he was unlike anyone Thomas had seen before, but then he had never seen a Jew. His hair was long and wild and a lock hung either side of his face. These were the horns that Thomas had seen. His flowing robes were dark with two tablet-shaped strips of yellow cloth sewn into them. He raised two reddish ovals of glass to his eyes and peered at Thomas.

'I am sorry for frightening you, young man. But your own appearance through the door rather startled us. Did it not, Hannah?'

He looked down at the young girl. She continued to look at Thomas, but nodded her agreement. Seeing Thomas's puzzlement at her father's actions with the glass, she smiled and explained.

'Father is short of sight. The glass is shaped to bend the light into his eyes.'

Thomas remained puzzled, and began to wonder again if this creature was after all a Devil's familiar. No girl he knew of could talk of such matters. Still, she seemed human enough –

indeed he could feel the warmth of her leg pressed against his thigh as he lay on the floor. Suddenly aware that he was still prostrate, he scrambled up and apologized for his abrupt entry. The girl rocked back on her haunches, looking up at him in amusement.

'Hannah, might I suggest you take our guest to the kitchen and find him something to eat and drink? It will give him time to gather his wits.'

Thomas was about to protest when he felt Hannah's warm, soft hand slip into his. He allowed himself to be led down the corridor, enticed by the swish of Hannah's dress and the slap of her feet on the stone flags. Passing a door to his right, his nose was assaulted by a variety of bewildering smells he could not place. Some of them reminded him of the countryside he had so recently left, others smelled of nothing he had ever encountered before. Looking through the open doorway, he was aware of a dimly lit room in which sparkled rows of vials and bottles set on shelves all around. Hannah's insistent grip dragged him on however. As she led him through into the kitchen he glanced over his shoulder to see the old man disappearing into the room clutching a vial. It was from this that Thomas had seen the smoke of hell emanating when he had fainted.

She had explained as Thomas ate that her father was a doctor with a wide knowledge of herbs and medicines. It was as she spoke that Thomas had become fascinated by her lips. Now his embarrassment was covered by a familiar voice at the other end of the corridor. There were hurried footsteps and the figure of Master Falconer appeared in the doorway. Any show of relief that flitted across his face was covered by the brusqueness of his voice.

'You young fool. You might have been killed.'

Shame at being so called in front of Hannah made Thomas respond in a way he would not normally have dared to one so senior as his Oxford Master.

'I can take care of myself. I travelled here to Oxford when a whole army could have been the end of me. I am not afraid of a few town traders.'

Falconer was inclined to reply in kind, but noted the tremor in the boy's voice. He noted too the sideways glance Thomas gave to the pretty girl sitting at his elbow. His actual response was conciliatory.

'Anyway, you are safe. And well fed by the look of it. If the hue and cry has died down, perhaps we can now return to the hall. Curse the murderer of that poor girl.'

He looked with some embarrassment at Hannah and apologized for his outburst.

'No need to apologize,' she said. 'I too could wish to curse him. You see, I knew her.'

His sleep was disturbed by thoughts of his father – the face curiously serene as the sword cleft it in two. Then suddenly he was floating over his own body, tossing restlessly on the narrow mattress. He saw his own face contorted with anguish, and he knew he was dreaming of his father's death. Rivulets of tears poured down his cheeks, and his mouth twisted in a silent scream. He thought he saw his tongue poking out of his mouth, but it was green and had eyes. He realized it was a lizard crawling out of his own body. He watched entranced as it scurried down the blanket to the floor and disappeared in a corner of the room. A sudden fear gripped him as he recalled the story his father had told him as a child. A sleeping man had nearly lost his soul, appearing in the shape of a lizard, when someone had tried to prevent it returning to his body before he woke. Immediately he was back inside his body and awake, shaking with fear. Without really knowing why, he crawled on his knees into one corner of the room, hunting for something he was convinced he had lost. Inside he just felt empty.

Chapter Six

Thomas de Cantilupe had been chancellor of the university for only two years, but in that time the cases appearing before the chancellor's court had increased to such a point that he was no longer able to deal with them all himself. Today he had settled the case of a Master falsely accused of being a Scotsman, had made a friar swear not to make suspicious visits to a tailor's wife, and now he had to talk to Master Falconer about interfering in a simple case of murder. It was not, after all, a member of the university who had been killed. And he had the aftermath of yesterday's riot to cope with and whether to call down the wrath of the King on the town. If indeed the King was in any position to command anyone in his realm.

The chancellor hurried from the chilly hall where the court was held. He scratched hard at his back. Why was the itch always in a place he could not reach? He eagerly cast off his academical cope, its tear now carefully repaired, and wrapped himself in the brown fur gown left over the back of his favourite chair. He drew himself up to the fire and poured a generous amount of red wine into a pewter tankard. Try as he might he could not imagine his interview with Falconer would go smoothly. He was a stubborn man and an Aristotelian. What was it he was fond of calling himself? A deductive. Well his days of demonstration must be curbed. He felt another itch between his shoulder blades and rubbed his back against his chair. Swallowing the last of the wine, he called his servant.

'Halegod!'

A short, stooping man scuttled into the room and stood in reverential silence.

'Is Master Falconer here?'

The servant affirmed that Falconer had been waiting some time. De Cantilupe sighed. No doubt the man would now be more irascible than usual.

'Send him in. And bring some food, and more wine.'

Halegod turned and left with the same scuttling gait. Unlike his master he was pleased to have made the visitor wait. It merely served to emphasize his own importance as servant to the chancellor of the university. Still, the towering Master could clearly be the sort to lose his temper and kill someone. Like Halegod. He imagined those big peasant hands closing around his windpipe and hurried into the small room where he had made Falconer wait and almost collided with the big man. A strangled cry came from his lips.

'I heard you coming,' said Falconer, by way of explanation. 'Is the chancellor free? I have things to do.'

Recovering his composure, Halegod asked Falconer to follow him.

The chancellor was still absently rubbing his back against the wing of his chair when Falconer was left by the servant at the entrance to the warm and well-appointed room. Bright wall-hangings served a practical as well as decorative purpose, keeping the chill of another February day at bay. Falconer coughed and de Cantilupe abruptly stopped his rubbing and turned his look to the doorway.

'Master Falconer. Come in and sit by the fire.'

The voice sounded to Falconer to be full of false bonhomie, which did not bode well for the interview.

'I have instructed Halegod to bring some food and more wine. I trust you will join me.'

Falconer was convinced this was going to be unpleasant. The chancellor's thin face with its hooked Roman nose was the face of an ascetic. Yet he was a man of contradictions; with a delight in good food and the flushed cheeks of a lover of wine. Stranger still that his lectures on the Scriptures were outstanding, and that he was inclined to wearing a hair shirt. Falconer suddenly realized he was being asked a question.

'My apologies, Chancellor.'

'I asked if you were proposing to pursue the case of that murdered servant girl. She is, after all, the business of the town constable. And I would have thought your attention would be fully occupied by keeping your students out of mischief. I hear one of them was lost in Jewry.'

Falconer was appalled that de Cantilupe had heard of his minor affairs and began his excuses. Fortunately Halegod came into the room with a large platter of cold beef, fowl, cheese and another large flagon of red wine. The regent master, used to simpler choices, stopped his reply. The older man took his hesitancy as acquiescence, breathing a sigh of relief at diverting Falconer so easily.

'I am glad we see eye to eye on this matter. We do not want a repeat of the last reason for your attaining notoriety.'

Once again Falconer began to present his excuses, but saw it would be simpler to keep quiet. He would continue with the murder matter until his deductive reasoning led him to a satisfactory conclusion, but would now do it more discreetly. Anyway, hadn't the previous chancellor congratulated him on finding the murderer of the Papal Legate's cook? Notorious, indeed.

*　　*　　*

Thomas was getting tired of Hugh Pett's constant surveillance of his every move. As he crossed the small room he now shared with the older boy at Falconer's insistence, he was conscious of Hugh's eyes tracking him. It was not even as though Hugh enjoyed his task. Every move of Thomas's clearly annoyed his companion and brought forth an irritated sigh. This last expulsion of air brought a retort from Thomas.

'If everything I do annoys you so much, then leave me.'

'You know, farmer's boy, that he has told me to keep an eye on you. And until the town has settled down and lectures start again – if they do – I will do just that.'

Thomas was angered by the richer boy's reference to his background, but was still too unsure of himself to answer back. Anyway, Hugh immediately regretted his taunt, and tried to soften it.

'At least you are not a Northern foreigner,' he grudgingly added.

'Or a Scotsman,' returned Thomas, with a laugh.

'Heaven forbid!'

Hugh's hand rested lightly on Thomas's shoulder; the young boy felt a shiver run through him. Hugh quickly drew his hand away, but still stared into Thomas's eyes.

'It is dangerous, you know.'

'What?'

'To go out and about. Even in daylight, as now. The story is that some students have been killed by townies. And the last time that happened the university closed down for a year until the King himself punished the town.'

Thomas groaned. The university not operating for a year and him only just arrived. The thought of returning to corn and chickens filled him with despair. Besides he wanted to see Hannah again. She had said she knew the murdered girl and if he could find out something more about her from Hannah, perhaps he could get back into Master Falconer's good books. The Master was, after all, seemingly intrigued by the death. But first he had to get rid of Hugh Pett. Perhaps boredom would induce him to give up his vigil. Thomas yawned hugely, lay back on the thin blanket spread on his hard pallet and closed his eyes. After a while there was another huge sigh from his companion. This was going to take some time.

The chancellor was beginning to wish that he had not decided to deal with Falconer gently. It was definitely going to take an effort to divert him from investigating the death of the servant girl. Especially as he was clearly enjoying the food before him. Falconer wiped his mouth and continued his explanation.

'It is the "Prior Analytics" that clearly show the theory of deduction. Two general truths, not open to doubt, often imply a third truth of more limited scope.'

De Cantilupe sighed.

'And what do you infer from the death of the servant girl?'

'I infer nothing from her death.'

De Cantilupe opened his mouth to end the interview on this acquiescence, but Falconer ignored the older man and continued. He was now well into his stride, and changed the emphasis of the statement.

'It is what I infer about her death and its manner that is intriguing. You see, her throat was cut at an angle and there was bruising on her right arm only.'

Here he paused, and clearly expected the chancellor to use his own powers to draw a conclusion. Halegod sidled into the room to clear the remains of the repast just as his master had to admit he did not see what these facts led to. Halegod's impassive stare turned into one of fear as Falconer grasped him from behind and held him by the throat.

'If you attack from behind, the natural move is to put your arm around the torso and draw the knife across your victim's neck.'

Halegod squawked as Falconer drew a table-knife across his windpipe.

'The resultant cut would be level. On the other hand . . .'

Halegod did not trust Falconer to repeat the demonstration with his neck leaving it unscathed. He twisted from the Master's grip and scuttled off, still clutching the greasy platter he had picked up.

'On the other hand, if you confronted your victim, grabbed her arm and drew a knife across her neck, the cut would be at an angle. I deduce that the victim knew her killer and it mattered not to him that she saw his face. He probably intended to kill her. She was too frightened even to fight back. There was no blood on her fingernails.'

Falconer's face was alight with his exposition to the older man. He stood over him grasping each arm of the large chair where the chancellor sat. Unfortunately his enthusiasm was not shared. De Cantilupe stared back at Falconer wearily.

'And where does this get you, Master?'

Falconer hesitated. He respected de Cantilupe, but sometimes the man did not understand that the truth derived from one deductive inference could serve as the premise for another set of inferences. He simply did not have all the truths to deduce the final, important fact. Not yet, anyway.

Again de Cantilupe took Falconer's silence as agreement that the older man was right. He was about to dismiss Falconer, when Halegod appeared in the doorway only to be bundled aside by the tense figure of Master de Stepyng. His pale face was set in a rigid mask of disapproval.

'Chancellor, we must take swift action against the town. The King must be petitioned.'

De Cantilupe sighed. 'The student deaths are regrettable.'

De Stepyng's thin mouth set into a tighter line at the chancellor's choice of words, but the older man persisted.

'But I fear the state of the country outside these walls means that the loss of three students is the least of the King's concerns.'

Falconer's gaze turned on the chancellor, a puzzled look in his eyes, but before he could ask where the third student had been killed, de Stepyng snorted in disgust.

'Our good and noble King Henry concerns himself too little with the urgent matters of true Englishmen. Surrounding himself with alien French has brought the country to this extremity.'

'My dear man, are you taking sides? I understand your own mother was French, and I remind you that de Monfort is himself French.'

The chancellor's retort did not stop the fastidious little Master, whose reply was turned to the onlooker to this argument.

'Falconer, you at least must see that the country's future lies in compliance with the provisions made in this very city.'

It was a statement rather than a question, but Falconer favoured it with a reply nonetheless.

'A Parleyment of barons may help to advise the King, but he still is our King.'

He paused, and turned the conversation to his own purpose.

'I am however most interested in the third student to die. You see, I myself witnessed the death of two of them on the edge of Jewry. Where was the third found?'

De Stepyng's face turned sour, and he spat out the answer.

'At the doors of my hall. He was one of my own students – Moulcom the Northerner. I found him in the early hours sprawled on the steps. So close to safety.'

'May I see his body? Where is it now?'

The chancellor did not like the light in Falconer's eye. Far from warning him off investigating one death, he had unwittingly involved him in a second. The food he had so recently relished now lay like a cold leaden lump in his stomach.

'For the moment he is in my hall. I will take you to him if you wish, though what you hope to achieve by looking, I do not know.'

De Stepyng's cold look turned on the unfortunate chancellor.

'What we now need is firm action against the whole town. They are all guilty.'

Thomas was at last making his way back into Jewry. It had taken a long time to lull Hugh Pett into believing he was asleep. But eventually the boy had left the room, giving Thomas time to hoist himself out of the window. The drop had been chancy, but he was used to climbing out of the upper window back at the farm in order to seek some peace for himself. How distant his life on the farm now seemed. His father had little time for him except as a labourer, yet here he now was, a student in Oxford, making his way to talk to a Jewess about a murdered girl. The rain of the previous day had now turned to ice on this cold afternoon. It crackled underfoot, and occasionally Thomas slipped, clutching the walls lining the lane for support. His breath came in white clouds which reminded him of the mists on the evening of the murder. He had to pass the spot where the murder took place, but knew no other route to Jewry. Fortunately there was no one about, so he bowed his head and hurried on.

*   *   *

The body lay on a table in the chilly hall. Unlike the body of the girl that Falconer had examined earlier, no loving care had been exercised over Moulcom. He was, however, once again in the company of Peter Bullock. The squat town officer had been waiting at de Stepyng's door when the two Masters had arrived. He had asked to see the body although he had no jurisdiction over the university. He said it was to satisfy himself of the cause. This had incensed de Stepyng, who once again began his tirade against the town. At least with his anger vented, he had left Falconer and Bullock in peace to examine the body.

Moulcom's head lay turned away from the door, his arm carelessly hanging over the edge of the table. Bullock gave the corpse a cursory glance and sighed.

'A tally of three, then.'

He turned to leave as Falconer moved around the table to get a better look, and was stopped by an exclamation from the other man. Falconer was peering intently at the face. 'Look at this, my friend.'

Bullock crossed the room and stood beside Falconer. The face that had been turned away from them on entering was black and the eyes protruded in a ghastly stare.

'This man has not been beaten to death as the others were,' said Falconer.

Bullock grunted in acknowledgement. 'No, obviously he was hanged, also not unusual in the circumstances.'

Falconer merely shook his head, and grasping Bullock's arm pulled his face close to the corpse's. The stench of death invaded his nostrils.

'Look. The marks on the neck are not those made by a rope. He has been strangled. Tell me if that is common, in the circumstances!'

Bullock had to grudgingly admit that he had never seen a

person strangled in the many pitched battles between students and townsfolk. Injuries were usually inflicted on the spur of the moment, not in any premeditated way. He failed to see where that led, however, and told Falconer so.

'Neither do I,' he admitted. 'But I am sure he was not killed as a result of the rioting. This was done for a reason, and may be linked with the girl's death. The killer simply used the riot as a convenient means of shifting the blame.'

'What proof have you?'

Falconer sighed.

'None, but it is merely a case of collecting sufficient truths.'

Bullock reached up with a work-worn hand and patted the taller man on the shoulder.

'You're far beyond me in this matter.'

He turned away and made for the door with his lurching gait. His last remark was thrown over his shoulder almost as a reprimand to the Master.

'I am merely charged with tidying up after the event.'

The remark was lost on Falconer who was closely examining the hands and clothing of the body, as though they would tell him who had killed Moulcom. Bullock slammed the door and left the scholar to his fancies.

Thomas had been worried about finding Hannah again, but in fact she found him. They now sat together in a chamber of her father's house as she explained that no one moved around Jewry without it being known. Care was the watchword, especially in these troubled times when it was known Earl Simon hated the Jews more than the King. At least the Jews were of use to the monarch. Thomas had not been aware that Joshua had dogged his footsteps ever since he crossed the invisible line that marked the beginning of the Jews' domain in Oxford. He had merely blundered around, trying to find the door through which he had fallen the previous day – but then he was being chased and had paid no heed to where he was.

Turning a corner in the maze of alleys, he was therefore surprised to be confronted by Hannah herself standing next to a young Jew. The man's cold eyes had a maturity belying the fuzz of beard growth on his chin and they shone with resentment of Thomas's presence. Hannah told Joshua that it was all right, that she was safe, and he reluctantly disappeared into the shadows. Thomas was not certain, however, whether he was following as Hannah led him to her father's house. Leading him in, he was certain that he would not have recognized the door.

'I'm glad you found me.'

'So am I.'

She touched him lightly on his hand, and Thomas blushed. He blurted out the purpose of his visit to avoid any further embarrassment. Hannah's brown eyes widened as the boy explained his Master's interest in the death of Margaret Gebetz. When he asked her about knowing Margaret, she explained that the girl had often come to her father for remedies for Master John Fyssh. While she waited for the preparations she would talk to Hannah, although her English was imperfect.

'She often talked of her family's home village of Mirepoix, and seemed happy enough until a few weeks ago.'

'What happened?'

'I don't know what had happened to her, but she looked pale and scared. I asked her what was wrong, but she refused to talk. This went on for several visits. She just refused to talk, until last week.'

'Was she back to normal?'

'No, she looked even more afraid, but was anxious to confide in me.'

Hannah explained that Margaret had said she had a book and wanted Hannah to keep it safe for her. She said by way of explanation that it was proof, and there was someone in Oxford who was trying to take it from her. She had been reluctant to say who it was, and was clearly terrified of him. At that point Hannah's father had returned.

'Proof of what?'

'I don't know. She mumbled something to me as she left, but I cannot be sure what it was and I never saw her again, for she was killed only days later.'

A tear formed in the corner of Hannah's eye, and she leaned against Thomas for comfort. He felt the warmth of her body against his and tentatively put his hand on her leg, not daring to put his arm around her. For a few seconds he felt the joy of physical contact with this attractive girl. Then she recovered herself and sat up again. Thomas reluctantly withdrew his hand and wondered what use this information would be to Falconer.

'I've still got it, of course.'

'What?'

'The book Margaret gave me. I'll fetch it.'

She swept out of the room with Thomas trying to imagine the body beneath the heavy folds of her dress. He realized that he had more than one motive in seeking her out in the first place. However, if he did not concentrate on the matter in hand, he knew he would not only appear foolish to Hannah but would not have helped his Master.

Hannah returned with a battered little book bound in red leather. She offered it to Thomas, who took it and flicked through the stained pages. He could tell some of it appeared to be scripture, but another part was a book of days. Why had it been so important to Margaret Gebetz, and more so to her persecutor, who was presumably also her murderer? He turned to inside the front cover hoping to find a title, but there was nothing but some spidery indecipherable handwriting. There was, however, something very familiar to a farmboy used to the butchery of animals. Across the first page and spreading down the edge of the book was the dark brown stain of blood.

Chapter Seven

After two days of pressure from regent masters like Robert de Stepyng, the chancellor decided to convene the powerful group of Masters of the arts known as the Black Congregation. A decision was needed concerning a suitable punishment for the town after their excesses during the riot. St Mildred's church was cold and depressing in the early morning, but it did not seem to quench the ardour of some Masters. Falconer sat on one of the benches to the back of the church, as Master after Master, like black crows at a corpse, rose and flapped their arms to emphasize their case. Justice must be brutal to be remembered. It mattered not a jot that several houses belonging to townspeople had been put to the flame. After all, three innocent students had been killed.

'Two,' muttered Falconer, but only his nearest neighbour heard him in the hubbub. It was Master Bonham, and he gave Falconer a curious look before rising to his feet and leaving while the other crows still argued. A smug smile played across his lips.

Retribution and an appeal to the King may have been taxing the minds of the great and good in the university, but for many, scholarship was of greater importance. While the chancellor considered how to restore the town to its proper subservient position, dependent on the university for its livelihood, lectures to the student body were starting up again. For Thomas this was the beginning of a new experience and he drank in everything about it.

Master Falconer had deemed Thomas's skill in grammar sufficient that he could proceed to lectures in the other two parts of the trivium, which made up the first part of a student's course. These were rhetoric and logic and would be expounded in Latin. Thomas was glad of Henry Ely's help in his studies before coming to Oxford.

Hugh Pett had guided him to the crowded little schools behind St Mary's church, a little angry that Thomas had once again escaped his attentions the other day. But not ungrateful that he had returned safely before their Master found out. Hugh left him at the door of the rhetoric school. He had already progressed to the quadrivium and was not keen to be seen with the lower mortals.

Thomas pushed open the door of the lecture room to be confronted by bedlam. It may have only been the sixth hour of the morning, but the room was crowded with young students wide awake and full of the activities of the last few days. The cacophony of raised voices echoed around the bare stone walls. The unglazed windows and plain floors should have given the room a cold and grim appearance. But the riot of movement on the simple benches, arranged to face a desk set high on a wooden stand, gave the lie to the grimness. Everyone knew the Black Congregation was meeting, and hoped their lectures might be cancelled or at least delayed. In the meantime everyone could relax. The talk itself was not all of death and retribution. Young minds did not focus on revenge for long, and many faces were split with grins as humorous exchanges were bandied between friendly rivals. A little relieved, Thomas felt he could perhaps enjoy this after all.

He smiled, then burst into laughter as one bench tipped over casting a dozen students to the ground in a heap. As the tangle of bodies sorted themselves out, the laughter around Thomas died and he realized the desk at the head of the room was now occupied. A small grey man had appeared at the desk as if from nowhere, and was silencing the crowded room with his disapproving gaze. Thomas joined the students who had recently tumbled from their bench in a more sober mood. Master Richard Bonham began, his voice thin and quiet, but somehow carrying around the room.

'Today I shall concern myself with judicial rhetoric. I shall summarize each text before proceeding to it in substance. I shall then give you a clear and explicit statement of each law. Then I shall read each text with a view to correcting it. Fourthly I shall repeat the contents of each law and fifthly solve any apparent contradictions, adding any general principles of law developed therefrom.'

For Thomas the hard work had begun.

Falconer was also working hard. The Jewish girl had said she had known the murdered Margaret Gebetz, and perhaps there was something to cull from her memory. He had sent word to Samson, asking that his daughter come to his rooms with a yarrow remedy to cure a toothache. He indeed did have an aching tooth, but the greater reason for asking for the remedy was to speak to Hannah without her father present to distract her. He felt she would speak more freely that way. While he awaited her arrival, he puzzled once again over the jigsaw of bones before him. The larger ones were clearly human and eclipsed the others, which a country boy such as Thomas would have recognized as a large bird's. Bones from both groups had been carefully cut in half and Falconer was examining their interior.

It was several years now since he had spoken to Friar Bacon about the flight of birds and his conviction that man could emulate them. He looked at Balthazar, the owl, perched quietly in the corner of his room. He had spent hours outside the city walls watching him skim across the fields and over the Thames. His effortless flight, with barely a flap of his wings, filled him with envy. He now knew why man could not hope to flap wings and fly in exactly the same way as birds. His self-appointed task lay in another approach – a machine for flight. As if in mockery, Balthazar lazily stretched his wings to their fullest extent and fixed Falconer with his unblinking stare. The man's consideration of the bird was interrupted by a light knock at his door.

He strode to it expecting Hannah. She was indeed there, but the old-young face of Joshua gazed coldly from over her shoulder. Falconer's questioning look elicited an answer from Hannah.

'My father thought it would still be dangerous for me to walk alone in the town.'

'Well, you are safe now.'

Falconer let the girl pass beneath his arm holding the door open, and abruptly slammed it in the face of her shadow before he could object. He turned back to the startled Hannah.

'Forgive me. My toothache makes me irritable.'

Hannah handed him a small pot.

'In the circumstances this may be doubly useful.'

He looked at her in puzzlement and she smiled.

'Yarrow is also said to be effective in curing the bite of a mad dog. When you open the door again, you may need it.'

As he made his way back to his lodging, Thomas had more to puzzle over than the subject of the lecture that he had struggled to follow as the pedantic Master Bonham worked his way through judicial rhetoric. Thomas had found his flat, monotonous tones more conducive to sleep than concentration. He had then been startled by the sudden noise at the end of the lecture as the other students rose from their benches. His neighbour pushed him, urging him to leave and Thomas apologized and stepped to one side. He wanted to remain in the hall and ask something of Master Bonham, if he dare pluck up the courage. The Master sat at his raised desk staring coldly at the students as they shuffled out of the room. It appeared no one dare make a noise until they exited the chamber. But Thomas could hear a relieved hubbub of conversation from beyond the door, and did not doubt that everyone was picking up their tales of rioting and death started prior to the lecture.

He had not heard the silent approach of Bonham, and was startled by the sharp voice at his shoulder.

'The lecture is over and I have to lock the chamber, boy.'

Thomas decided not to be put off by the cold tones. He had spent two days trying to decipher the contents of the book given to Hannah by the dead girl. If he could discover what the book was or why it was important, he hoped to restore himself in Falconer's favour. Master Bonham was the only other source of knowledge he could tap at present. He followed on the Master's heels and stood patiently as he locked the door.

'Sir, I need some help with a book.'

'Whose student are you? Go to the Master of your hall if you are too dull to construe a simple text.'

Thomas gulped, but pressed on. He drew the strange book from the folds of his tunic and thrust it at Bonham. As he did so, he fumbled and the book fell open on the ground. The teacher was about to turn away, when his eyes fell on the page. A strange look came over his normally blank face and he snatched the battered volume from the ground. He quickly leafed through it, then snapped it shut.

'Where did you get this?'

Somehow Thomas felt he should not reveal the truth of its origin, and stammered something about finding the book in the street after the riots.

'Then it is not your book to keep. I shall keep it myself until its rightful owner is found.'

Thomas had stood dumbfounded as the one tangible clue to the murder of Margaret Gebetz was whisked away by the little grey Master, his bald head bobbing down the street in his hurried departure.

Now, as Thomas turned into Aristotle's hall, he began to wonder if there was something to Bonham's desire to possess the book. He had appeared disinterested until his eyes had latched on to the book itself. What was so important about the book? Thomas thought he had better go straight to Falconer with the puzzle.

Meanwhile, Falconer had had no difficulty steering the conversation round to the topic of the murdered servant girl. His reputation for deductive reasoning, and interest in curious deaths encouraged Hannah herself to enquire if he had come to any conclusions. Falconer stated his belief that she had been killed by someone known to her, without detailing the gruesome evidence of the girl's slit throat. But he was more interested in what Hannah could tell him about the girl. He took care not to press her as she sat reflectively staring into the low glow of the fire. Her ivory skin took on the reddish glow and Falconer merely prompted her as she spoke.

It was clear that Margaret Gebetz had been a country girl from the Pyrenees, but Hannah did not know why she had left her village to be employed as a servant in Paris. It had been there at the university that Master John Fyssh had first employed her. She had been retained by him when he returned to the university at Oxford half a year ago. Hannah had little further information as Margaret was quiet and reserved and spoke little English. She seemed, anyway, to live in fear of her master.

'This cannot help now she is dead.' The girl's soft brown eyes turned to the man sitting in the shadow of the chimney breast, his face partially obscured.

'On the contrary, all facts, when properly understood, will inevitably reveal the crucial fact of the murderer's identity. Go on.'

Hannah shuddered as the wind howled down the chimney and blew a cloud of smoke into the room. She drew her cloak tighter around her and continued telling Falconer much of what she had already confided to Thomas; that she had got to know Margaret because Fyssh imagined he suffered from a variety of ailments and her father's skills were regularly called upon. Much of it was imagined. Fyssh often complained of sleeplessness and asked for a particular mixture made from poppy flowers. Margaret also ran many errands for Fyssh in his discourses with other Masters.

It had been only a short while before her death that Margaret had rushed in one day as though the Devil had been following her. She said she'd left Mirepoix to escape 'his kind', but when pressed would say no more. She had mumbled some words over and over again under her breath. And it had been only a day or so later that she had entrusted the book to Hannah. Falconer's face came sharply out of the shadow, his eyes screwed up as he squinted at the girl. Excitement at a crucial clue often caused him to forget to cover up his poor sight.

'Book? You mentioned no book to me. What book?'

Standing outside the door of Falconer's chamber, Thomas heard this exchange and groaned. He would have to explain how he had lost the book now. As he went to knock at the door, he heard Falconer continue.

'And the words she mumbled. Could you understand them?'

Hannah grimaced. 'I'm not sure, but I think she spoke of a good man. I can recall that because it seemed odd that she should speak of a good man when she was so frightened.'

'A good man? Are you sure it was those very words?'

Hannah looked into Falconer's searching gaze.

'Yes, I'm certain. Of course, she said it in her own language – *bon homme*.'

Thomas's clenched fist poised short of the door. Hearing what Hannah said were the girl's last words, he was suddenly sure he knew it was not a good man that Margaret was referring to, but someone by name. Regent Master Bonham's interest in Margaret's book was suddenly clear. He turned away and quietly slipped out of Aristotle's hall, concentrating so much on the idea of solving the murder before Falconer that he was unaware of the slim shadowy figure of Joshua following him.

Falconer now felt he was on his way to a solution of the girl's murder. Now he needed to provide the link with the student's death. Something about Moulcom was eluding him, and he was on his way to talk to Peter Bullock, having accompanied Hannah back to Jewry. Both had been a little curious at Joshua's disappearance, especially as Hannah said he was her self-appointed watchman, following her everywhere. Aware of her beauty, Falconer was not surprised. Still, her information about the murdered girl was interesting and he was sure that when he saw the book facts would fall into place. He merely had to wait until Thomas returned from his lectures, for the girl had told him his new student now possessed the book. Annoying that probably so vital a piece of information had been under his roof all the time. In the meantime, he wanted to verify something about the death of the Northerner. Was his death in fact linked to the girl's? For Falconer was sure he had not died as a result of the riots. And he himself had seen Moulcom leaving Beke's Inn just before the riots began.

Bullock lived at the end of Great Bailey in the shadow of the keep at the west of the city. His house was shadowy too, as though he wished to hide his bent back from public sight. Bullock opened the door to Falconer's insistent knocking. Falconer did not expect to be allowed into the other man's house – he jealously guarded his private domain. Or perhaps he did not trust anyone from the university. Even Falconer. The regent master came straight to the point.

'Moulcom, the Northerner's clothes. Do you recall whether they were wet or not?'

Bullock sighed, for he was used to these strange whims of Falconer's. He could never follow where they were going, but they often seemed to lead to an important conclusion.

'All the dead students' clothes were wet – they had lain in the rain.'

'Yes, but Moulcom's – were they wet all over?' Falconer persisted.

Bullock stood and thought, his hand holding the door close to his body defensively.

'The front of his clothes was wet. I remember from when I picked him up in the street.'

'And the back?'

'Dry, I think. But——'

'Thank you. That is as I recalled it, but I wanted to be sure.'

Falconer turned to go, but Bullock, his curiosity roused, put a hand on his shoulder. 'But the front of his clothes would be wet, he was found face down in the street.'

'And the other students' clothes?'

Bullock thought, briefly. 'Were wet all over because they had lain in the rain. So Moulcom was killed later, after the rain had stopped.'

Falconer stared into Bullock's face in excitement, as his deductive logic led him to its conclusion.

'But the rain persisted all night. Indeed that's what cooled the anger of the rioters. No one was on the rampage in the morning when the rain finally stopped.'

'And Moulcom was killed in the morning?'

'Perhaps. I am more inclined to think he was killed in the safety and seclusion of someone's home and his body dumped in the street to shift the blame.'

Thomas learned that Master Bonham lived somewhere near St Michael's at North Gate. He had decided he would retrace his steps from his lecture and get to the north wall of the city via Schools Street. Once there he felt sure someone could tell him exactly where to find Bonham, even in such a teeming city as Oxford. On the corner of Schools Street stood the church of St Mary's which was in process of being rebuilt on a grander scale to reflect its central nature to the university. For the present it was merely a building site, the church cocooned in poles and ropes, and surrounded by apparently haphazard piles of stone. Turning past the church, Thomas thought he saw someone step underneath the criss-cross of wooden scaffolding that covered the church's north side. The figure seemed to be beckoning, although no one else was working on the tower. Thomas looked around, thinking the workman was signalling to someone else. But there was no one. The figure beckoned again, pointing directly at Thomas, while still standing in the shadows of the tower.

Thomas stepped across the jumble of stones at the base of the workings and called out.

'What do you want?'

The person could not have heard him because he moved out of sight under the half completed north tower of the church. Reaching the archway under which the figure had gone, Thomas looked around but could no longer see him. Deep shadows obscured the base of the tower, which was still open to the elements. Thomas looked up to the dull grey sky, and thought he saw someone on the stone parapet above his head. A thin trickle of dust on to his upturned face confirmed it. The elusive nature of the person reminded him of the half-glimpsed shape leaving the body of Margaret Gebetz, and Thomas shuddered at the thought.

He called out, in the hope that the other man would respond, and all would be harmlessly resolved. Instead his voice echoed up the shaft of the tower, and Thomas felt worse than before. At that point he was sure he should turn back and continue his search for Bonham. But then he thought he heard his own name being whispered from above.

'Hello, who's there?'

Once again his name drifted on the wind from above. He nervously wrapped his jerkin around him and started up the stone staircase that was built into the thickness of the wall to his left. He cautiously made his way up, stumbling over the chippings left by the masons who were working on the facing of the wall. As he emerged at the top, the wind blew in his face. The staircase ended abruptly, and the top of the tower had no protecting parapet. It was just a flat surface and a sheer drop off the edge. The wooden scaffolding looked very flimsy at this height. He stood still within the stairwell, and looked around. To his right the blocks making the next stage of the tower rose higher than the floor level he was on. He could not see anyone near him. The elusive figure must be hiding behind these higher stones. He would have to climb out on to the unprotected ledge.

He was still on his knees climbing out of the stairwell, when his jerkin was roughly grasped and he felt himself dragged to the very edge of the drop. He looked over his shoulder and gasped. The ground seemed a very long way away. Even climbing trees around his father's farm had not taken him this high, and the jumble of masonry below would be far harder than any grassy bank to land on. He turned to look at his assailant with pleading in his eyes. He stared into the implacable features of Joshua.

Chapter Eight

Thomas felt the collar of his jerkin being twisted tighter in the grip of the stronger man. If he didn't fall off the tower to his death, he would surely soon be strangled. He wriggled desperately under the weight of his assailant, but Joshua was too strong. Anyway, he could feel the edge of the building in the middle of his back now, cutting across his spine. If he moved again, they might both plunge to their deaths. He clutched at the joint in the stonework down by his waist, tearing his fingernails. The Jew thrust his face at Thomas and hissed into his ear.

'Hannah is not to be spoiled by you. You will leave her alone, one way or another.'

As he spoke, Thomas felt the weight of the other man's body relax. It was now or never, and he thrust up with his hips. Surprised by the move, Joshua loosened his grip on Thomas's clothes and began to slide over his shoulder. Thomas kicked up with his legs, completing the move, and desperately pulled himself from the precipice. With a cry of astonishment, Joshua somersaulted over Thomas's body and straight over the edge. There was a rending crash and silence.

Gasping, Thomas rolled over and dragged himself again to the edge. He peered down below him, fearing the worst for Joshua. There was a clutter of wooden poles directly beneath him; some were split and swinging free where Joshua had plunged. There was no sign of the body on the ground. Then he saw him.

Joshua was hanging by one hand to a firm piece of the scaffolding through which he had fallen. For a second his face, white and drawn, turned up to Thomas. Then he dropped the remaining distance to the ground. Thomas closed his eyes tight and ground his face into the stonework. Had he killed the man after all? He almost didn't dare look, and tears welled in his eyes. He could not bear to look once again over the drop, and dragged himself back to the well of the stairs. His legs were wobbly and unsteady as he descended, clutching the wall as he went. He felt cold and his breath came in gasps. At the bottom he stood in the archway for an age before he could thrust himself forward. He stepped carefully around the debris to the side of the tower where Joshua had fallen. There was no sign of him.

Unsure that he was in the right place, Thomas looked up and could discern the tangled mess of scaffolding through which Joshua had crashed. Ropes and poles still swung backwards and forwards above his head. The Jew must be inhuman to have survived such a fall. There was a rustling sound far off to his left. Peering into the gloom, he thought he saw some movement low down on the ground and saw a black cat scuttling away. Perhaps it was just a stray cat disturbed by all the noise. Or perhaps Joshua had altered his shape to escape death. Thomas shot a fearful glance over his shoulder, half expecting a demon to loom out of the darkness, but he was alone.

If Bullock had climbed the tower of the Great Keep under whose shadow he lived and peered west into the gloom of that winter's afternoon towards Beacon Hill, he might have seen the signs of an approaching army. From across the stream at the foot of the bailey and the woodland that approached the city walls came a curious sound. It could be discerned by the practised ear as the clash of metal on metal, the creak of leather and the thud of massed hoofs on the earth. These all mingled to produce a sound that could be likened to some fearful dragon heaving itself towards the city. In drier weather such an army would have raised a dust cloud resembling fiery dragon's breath and visible from many a mile. The recent persistent rain had soaked the soil, and slowed the progress of footsoldier and horseback-knight alike. From the top of the keep, it would have been possible to see a black and rolling mass moving across the open country like ants following their mindless brethren. Identifying the forces would have been difficult at this distance. If Bullock had been on the tower, he might have had some inkling of the army's leader from the small advance guard who burst out of the edge of the wood close to the keep. They wearily rode east around the city walls beyond the ditch and turned into the North Gate.

But Peter Bullock was not on the tower. He was still at home, staring into the dying embers of his fire and trying to fathom Falconer's thinking, and failing. In any case he had no place in national events. Let the King and the barons slaughter each other as long as they did not use Oxford as a battlefield.

The same lack of concern could not be attributed to the chancellor.

De Cantilupe was in a quandary. His better feelings made him sympathetic to the spirit of the Earl of Leicester's opposition to King Henry. After all, Earl Simon did not want to rule himself, merely prevent the King from ruling as a despot. The provisions agreed by the King in the chancellor's own city required him simply to rule reasonably well. There were many adherents to the barons' cause in the university and the town, not least the student body itself. On the other hand, the King had favoured the university on many an occasion and seemed to be planning to mass his forces at Oxford.

Now Henry's son Edward was due to arrive in Oxford shortly from the Welsh Marches. The chancellor's hair shirt prickled at the thought, and he began to absently scratch between his shoulder blades, contorting his body to achieve this feat. The stooping Halegod stood anxiously awaiting his orders, hopping from one foot to the other in front of the chancellor. De Cantilupe ignored him uncharitably.

How was he to handle the slippery Edward? Whose side was he on? You may have imagined that he stood firm with his own father. But only four years ago he had sided with Simon de Montfort when the earl had tried to hold the Candlemas Parliament in the absence of the King. At that time everyone had backed down, but who was to say that Edward would not switch sides again?

'Fetch Bonham – he will know where Edward stands. He always monopolizes the gossip from court.'

Halegod bowed obsequiously and scurried off to find Master Bonham. The chancellor returned to hunting the itch across his back.

Returning to his rooms after verifying the state of Moulcom's body with Bullock, Falconer began to review what he knew so far. He paced his room turning past the unmade bed and circling the table piled high with bones and books. His surroundings may have been in disarray, but he was practised in assembling information neatly in his mind. The high cost of paper and the poverty of his stipend resulted of necessity in this skill of his. Margaret Gebetz had been killed by someone she knew. She had also been frightened of someone or something in Oxford in recent months. She had asked Hannah to keep a book for her, a book now in Thomas's possession. Falconer pursed his lips in exasperation that there was still no sign of Thomas and so he could not pursue that matter. It may be that the book supplied the key to the puzzle. He continued his pacing oblivious to the cold of the room.

Moulcom had been strangled in someone's house, not by rioters in the street. He had last seen Moulcom leaving Fyssh's inn the day after the girl's death. The girl had worked for Fyssh. Was Fyssh the link between the two murders? Falconer sighed. That was an imaginative leap, not a deductive inference based on a comparison of all the known truths. It was unworthy of his Aristotelian tutelage. He slumped on to the edge of his bed and rubbed his weak eyes with the heels of his great spade-like hands. If only he could see more clearly. In both senses of the words.

A nervous cough brought him back to the present. Hugh Pett stood in the doorway of his room, anxiously twisting one sleeve of his rich green gown. His eyes were cast down to the floor and the oval of his fine red hair masked his look. Falconer was impatient at the interruption.

'Not now, Hugh.'

The student sighed and turned to go, but looked back at Falconer as he did so. Falconer was close enough to discern the paleness of the boy's face and immediately relented his curtness. He strode across the room and put his hand on the other's shoulder.

'Is there anything wrong?' he asked softly.

Hugh turned his face up to Falconer's with a hunted look in his soft brown eyes. The older man hesitated, seeing in that look a weakness in Hugh Pett's character he had come across before. Then he silently reprimanded himself for such a thought.

Who, least of all himself, was perfect in character? Especially at such an age as Hugh. He led the boy to a chair by the hearth and fussed about rebuilding the fire in it, appearing to deflect his attention from Hugh. As the kindling caught, Hugh stammered a few words.

'I wondered ... You see, I still feel guilty about letting Thomas loose the other day.'

Falconer blew on the small glow in the hearth, letting Hugh progress at his own pace. The boy continued, still nervously tugging at his sleeve, fraying the expensively embroidered edge.

'I thought I might help in some way.'

'You are, by continuing to keep an eye on him.'

'Yes, but I wondered if I could help solve the killing of the girl.'

Falconer could not help but burst into laughter. Then, before Hugh felt he had been callously rebuffed, explained that unfortunately he had no idea on the killer himself.

'Then you do not suspect Master Fyssh ... or anyone?'

Falconer narrowed his eyes. The boy had made the last statement with some rush of relief.

'Fyssh no more than anyone,' he qualified carefully.

Hugh Pett quickly rose from the chair and made across the room, hitting the table in his haste. He clutched at a large bone that slid towards the edge.

'Then I can be of no help?'

'Only as I said – to guide Thomas through his first days here.'

'Yes,' said Hugh with apparent relief. 'I'll do that. I promise you. I'll make sure he's back from schools and safe right now.'

The student disappeared down the creaky staircase, his now frayed sleeve flying behind him. Falconer was somewhat puzzled at his strange behaviour, but put it down to the boy's sense of guilt. Deductive logic now required his full attention. Either that or the fire, which was on the verge of failing.

Thomas sat on one of the great blocks of stone at the foot of the unfinished tower unsure of what to do next. The Jew had disappeared into the growing dark somehow. He could not entirely rid himself of the notion that the cat he thought he saw running away had been his assailant in another unholy guise. He shuddered at the thought, not least because it brought Hannah to mind. If he thought any Jew could change shape at will, did that not mean that she was in league with the Devil? He resolved to ask Falconer about the matter.

His problem now was what to do next. Should he still seek out Bonham? It was perhaps too late. Most people would be locking their doors against night prowlers, and he too should be safely in his room. The cold of the evening struck through him and he shivered. On the other hand he would have to face Falconer and report the loss of the book which seemed so important. Fear of his stern Master's rebuke was greater than fear of the dark. He got up and continued along Schools Street, his breath in cold mists around his lips. At the end of the street the high walls of the town loomed above him, casting even greater gloom along the lane running to right and left. North Gate was to his left and it was that way he decided to go.

Luck was on his side. He was halfway down the lane, walking in the shadow of the wall, when he saw a figure step out of a door only yards in front of him. It was Bonham himself – the primness of his posture and the grey garb were unmistakable. He turned back to talk to someone following him out of the doorway. A stooped old man emerged carrying a lantern to guide them through the dark. If they turned towards Thomas he would be seen. He saw a buttress of the outer wall a few feet away from him, and ran without thinking. He flattened himself into the scant protection the buttress afforded, his cheek pressed hard against the coarse stone. His breath came in great gasps and he thought he was bound to be revealed. However the voices of Bonham and his companion grew fainter. They were going the other way.

Thomas screwed up his courage to peer around the edge of the stonework. The lantern held aloft by the old man glinted on Bonham's bald head. They were disappearing into the murk towards North Gate. There was however another source of light in the lane. The weak light of guttering candles spilled out from the door of Bonham's house. He had failed to latch it properly in his haste to follow the man with the lantern. Thomas would never have a better opportunity to reclaim the book. He crossed the lane to the doorway and eased open the heavy oak door. There was no sound from inside, but Bonham might have students under his charge like Master Falconer. He slipped through the gap and closed the door carefully behind him. The hall was narrow and half blocked by a bound chest beside the door on which stood the candlestick whose light had beckoned Thomas. The candle flickered and died as he stood there, and his heart leapt as he was plunged into darkness.

Bonham was ushered into the chancellor's presence by the fussy Halegod, his lantern now extinguished and left at the door. De Cantilupe was eating some supper and he invited Bonham to join him. The little grey Master declined and stood patiently waiting for de Cantilupe to begin in much the same way as he waited for the students' attention in his lectures. The chancellor hesitated and popped another shred of meat into his mouth. Wiping his hands carefully with a clean white napkin, he chewed and swallowed before beginning.

'Master Bonham, you have your ear to the door of the royal court as much as anyone.'

The little man bobbed his head faintly in seeming acknowledgement, but said not a word.

'Prince Edward is due here shortly and I should like your opinion as to which breeze he bends with at the moment.'

Bonham paused before replying. No one, not even the chancellor, would dare say he hesitated. It was a considered pause.

'If I truly knew what was afoot in this dangerous world at present—'

The chancellor threw his hands up to confirm that he trusted Bonham's assessments implicitly. Bonham continued.

'If I truly knew, and if confrontation is inevitable as I believe it is, then the prince will favour the winning side.'

De Cantilupe sighed. Why was this tedious little man so pedantic?

'That does not help me in how to treat him when he arrives. The future of the university may depend on that.'

'Edward is the prince, and means to be King after his father.'

'And will he?'

Bonham clearly did not like direct questions.

'If you treat him as his rank deserves, no one can blame you afterwards. Whoever wins.'

'A banquet would not be inappropriate?'

Bonham treated the chancellor's question as rhetorical and turned to leave. De Cantilupe stared at his natural tonsure as he brushed the curtain aside and returned to absently picking morsels of meat from the now cold bone.

While Falconer absently poked at his flickering fire with a stick and pondered his next step, Hugh Pett was sneaking up the alley to Beke's Inn. He did not like what he was about to do for it taxed his loyalty to his Master. But other imperatives drove him to speak to Master John Fyssh. He stood irresolute at the door to Beke's Inn, but it opened abruptly before him and there stood John Fyssh himself, his jowls wobbling with anger.

'Come in before someone sees you.'

He grabbed the boy's arm and dragged him in, slamming the door behind him.

'I saw you coming. I've been waiting for an age. What have you been doing?'

The words tumbled one over the other, betraying Fyssh's anxiety.

'It was difficult – my Master is a clever man. And then I had to wait for dark like you told me.'

Fyssh softened but did not let go of Hugh's arm.

'Then tell me what you discovered. Does he suspect me?'

'No more than anyone, he said.'

'What sort of answer is that? That tells me nothing.'

Fyssh's eyes narrowed as another thought occurred to him.

'Did he ask you about a book the girl had?'

Hugh flinched as Fyssh squeezed his arm harder.

'A book? No,' was his puzzled reply. He hardly dared ask the question that then came to his lips.

'You didn't really kill her, did you?'

Fyssh sniggered, then released Hugh only to begin stroking his fine hair, brushing it away from his eyes.

'What if I did? You and I already have one little secret to keep from the rest of the world. You wouldn't want another, would you?'

Hugh was sure it was just false bravado on the other man's part. He could not see Fyssh as a killer. Cruel, yes, but his temperament fell short of murder. Still, he shuddered in the other's grasp, only gradually succumbing to his touch. Leaning against his shoulder, he just wished this had all not begun in the first place. Giving in to his feelings had now resulted in him betraying the only man he truly respected. He had felt released at first, now he just felt trapped.

Chapter Nine

There was no sound from the rest of Bonham's house, so Thomas edged along the passageway to the door at the end. It led straight into a small room lit red by the dying glow of a fire. Deep shadows were cast on the walls by a small stool and rickety table. The Master led a frugal life. A heavy wooden cupboard dominated one end of the tiny cell. Each shelf was stacked with books and papers. Thomas groaned at the thought of trying to find Margaret's book in such a heap, but it was the best place to start. He felt sure the book, so recently acquired, would not be at the bottom of a stack, so he scanned the top few spines of each pile. Some were texts even Thomas knew – Donatus' *Ars minor*, Pliny and Solinus – others were more anonymous items and seemed to be attributed to foreigners with names like Mondino and Berbuccio. Curious, Thomas took one from the top of the pile. The pages fell open naturally at the sketchy drawing of a naked male figure with text all around it. Lines led from the text to parts of the drawing, particularly the face. This was drawn in much more detail than the body, with a halo of hair. Horribly, the face was flayed of flesh as after some awful battle. The eyeballs were pulled out of their sockets and the mouth was nothing but leering teeth bereft of flesh. Thomas shuddered at such horror, and he became even more convinced of the murderous intent of the quiet little Master. He dropped the book back on the pile and continued his search. Unfortunately, the book he was seeking was not amongst these well-thumbed texts. He felt his way to the table by the fire. Perhaps the Master had been reading the book when he was called away. He looked down at the book lying open on the table and sighed in disappointment. It was too large to be the lost book. It appeared to be a book of recipes or cures. Thomas turned back to the beginning and mouthed the jumble of letters making up the title, *Meddygon Myddfai*.

Again it was meaningless to him – it was not even in Latin.

Another scan of the room gave him little hope of finding a hiding place for the book. Then he saw the small drawer under the lip of the table. He grasped the knob and pulled. There was something inside, wrapped in a cloth. He pulled it out – the shape was oblong, like the book. He carefully unwrapped the cloth to disclose a heavy leather case. It couldn't be the book, unless it was inside the case. He took a deep breath and untied the strap around the case. The case fell open to reveal an array of knives of curious shapes, and some of them were bloodied.

With trembling hands Thomas retied the cord on the case, wrapped it as before in the dirty cloth and returned the bundle to the drawer, praying each moment that Bonham would not return and discover him here. With the drawer closed, the room appeared undisturbed and Thomas was about to leave when he saw the closed book on the table. Bonham had left it open and would know someone had been in the room if he returned to find it not so. But where had he left it open at? Thomas seemed to remember it was a recipe against toothache, but how would he find it again? He feverishly flicked through the book and multicoloured illustrations jumped out at him. Beasts he knew like dogs and sheep, and stranger ones he had not seen before – red dragons and giant worms. But nothing that seemed to relate to toothache. In fear of being discovered, he simply left the book open and made his escape. Surely he now had something to offer Falconer in compensation for losing the book? At the door to the lane, he hesitated then pulled it open and peered into the dark. There was no one around, so he pulled the door closed behind him and returned the way he had come, assuming Bonham would himself return from the direction of North Gate.

The following morning started bright and clear, with the grey clouds of the last few days scattered by the high winds. The watery sun hung low just over the parapet of the city walls and shone down St John's Street into Falconer's room. He awoke early and decided he had contained his impatience with Thomas long enough. The boy had come back very late the previous night with an urgent tale for the Master. To teach him a lesson of patience, Falconer had refused to see him, and had insisted on his going to bed in penance for being out dangerously late. The nuisance was Falconer himself was impatient to see the book, and had had to learn the same lesson imposed on the boy.

The wind roared down the chimney, scattering ashes around the room. Falconer angrily wiped the grey dust from his books on the table and left to rouse Thomas. It was not necessary. Thomas was already awake and dressed, sitting anxiously on the single chair in the room he shared with Hugh Pett. Hugh was still abed, wrapped up against the cold currents that whistled through the door.

Before Thomas could speak, Falconer held out his hand and asked for the book given him by Hannah. Thomas hung his head and explained that he no longer had it, but that he had some other important information. Falconer simply ignored him and spun half-round in exasperation. The bright start to the day was getting dimmer.

'You have lost the book – no doubt the crucial clue to unravelling the truths of this matter?'

'Master Bonham took it. I could not refuse.'

Falconer grabbed Thomas's arm and guided him firmly out of the room. At the door he threw a comment over his shoulder to the apparently somnolent Pett.

'Let us leave noble Lord Pett to his dreams, and take the air.'

He purposely left the student's door open, and was glad to hear a groan from within as he crossed the hall to the front door. Thomas scurried after him. In the lane, Thomas wrapped his cheap toga around him. The sun promised more warmth than the strong winds allowed. Falconer seemed oblivious to the cold, his robes flapping out behind him as he strode along. Thomas knew better than to blurt out his discovery of yesterday just yet. He already realized that Master Falconer liked to discover his own truths, or at least appear to do so. He did feel he could ask a simple question, however.

'Where are we going?'

'Going? Why to Master Bonham's, of course.'

It was at that point Thomas realized he must tell Falconer the truth about his late-night exploit whatever the consequences.

And so it was that Falconer stood alone at Bonham's door with Thomas nowhere in sight. On being admitted by Bonham, Falconer apologized for the earliness of the hour but explained that he understood Bonham had taken a book from one of his students.

'His description aroused my curiosity. As you know, I have a weakness for puzzles. And I thought a look at it might help me place its origin.'

Bonham was about to answer when there was a thunderous

knocking at his door. The little grey man pursed his lips and, excusing himself, went to the door. There was no one there. He looked angrily to the left, then squinted into the sun to his right. He could not see clearly and stepped out of the doorway, shading his eyes. The wind swirled around an empty lane – it was still so early that no one was abroad at all. He returned to his room and the early morning arrival who had stayed long enough to be invited in.

'Some foolish student who thinks it funny to disturb me at this early hour,' he said tartly in response to Falconer's querying look.

'As for the book, you are too late. It was a useless jumble of peasant calendar lore. It did well to light my fire this morning.'

He was clearly reluctant to say more, but was sure Falconer would not be so easily put off. He was therefore relieved when the normally persistent Master abruptly thanked him and hurried to leave. As the door closed on Falconer, he shook his head in sad reflection on the butterfly nature of Falconer's mind.

As he strolled back down the lane, Falconer appeared to speak to thin air.

'You can come out now.'

Thomas emerged from behind the buttress which had provided him with cover the night before and from where he had played his trick with Bonham's knocker. He was grinning.

'Did you get it?'

'I am afraid the book eludes us at present.'

Thomas looked crestfallen.

'However, I used your timely distraction to do something else.'

He thrust his hand into his pouch and produced a small but extremely sharp knife, still with blood on the blade.

'You had time to take that?' asked Thomas incredulously.

'Barely. I was still closing the drawer when he returned.'

'Will it prove his guilt?'

'The Master is guilty of nothing at present. This is merely one element which will contribute to an understanding of the greater truth. If a bloodstained knife is evidence of guilt, then every man who slaughters beasts for the table is a murderer. For now, we will pursue the matter of the book in another direction.'

The town had begun to stir as they made their way back to Aristotle's hall. There was still a feeling of sullenness in the traders as they set up shop. But the abnormality of the last few days was receding as the need to earn money grew. Passing a butcher standing at a worn and heavily scarred block, Falconer paused as the man slit the belly of a rabbit and in a few strokes deftly peeled off its pelt, leaving the red carcass. He nodded with satisfaction, apparently at the man's skill, and continued on his way.

Meat, and its preparation, was also of concern to Thomas de Cantilupe. He needed to provide a banquet for Edward and was now learning the cost. Halegod stood before him, with the list of requirements from the cooks. The chief cook himself stood to the back of the room. Although his calling gave him an honoured position in the society of the well-to-do, it also made his presence less than desirable. De Cantilupe's fastidious nature was repelled by the smell of animal fat. Indeed the cook's pores seemed to drip like some roasting carcass. Halegod droned on holding the paper close to his rheumy eyes.

'The best goose – sixpence; the best rabbit without the skin – fourpence; the best dunghill mallard – twopence; the best curlew – sixpence.'

'Is there nothing less costly?'

Halegod scanned his list.

'A dozen finches – one penny.'

'I cannot serve the prince and the Black Congregation a dozen finches!'

Halegod gave the chancellor a sour look. He was clearly disappointed that, with such an opportunity for ostentation, only the regent masters of the arts – the Black Congregation – had been required to attend. The chancellor, however, had deemed it politic to steer a middle road. And expend a modest amount. It would appear that his hopes for the latter were to be dashed. De Cantilupe sighed and bowed to the inevitable.

'Do what you think necessary. And use some students to help serve. They will do it for a good meal and save some money for me.'

He waved his servant away, who in his turn ushered the cook out ahead of him, taking care not to soil his hands on the other's greasy garb. De Cantilupe's hope was that all the expense would be worth it in the long run. His sympathies lay with de Montfort; the problem was, where did Edward's lie?

The cold of the nave floor bit through Hugh's soft boots, and he shuffled uncomfortably from foot to foot. The heavy pillars of St Frideswide's seemed to press down on him, and he was on the verge of giving up when he heard the wheezing tones of Master John Fyssh. The heavy man entered by the south transept and turned towards the presbytery. He fell to his knees and bowed to the altar, his back to Hugh. He seemed bound up in prayer. Hugh nervously approached him, unsure whether to interrupt him or not. Fyssh's mutterings abruptly changed into an insistent hiss.

'Come, tell me what more information you have before we are discovered.'

Hugh self-consciously knelt beside him.

'I remembered you were interested in a book when we . . . met last.'

'Well?'

'My Master seems interested in a book also. One that belonged to the dead girl.'

Hugh recalled that this church was where Margaret Gebetz had been first brought and shivered. He went on.

'Another student had it, but it was taken from him by Master Bonham.'

'Is that all?' raged Fyssh as he hefted himself to his feet. 'I have interrupted a perfectly good dinner for this morsel?'

He turned away from the boy who bowed his head in fear. In that position he did not see the smile of satisfaction on Fyssh's face as he lumbered back down the south transept and out into the cloister.

Crossing the High Street, Falconer surprised Thomas by walking towards Jewry and not Aristotle's hall. The boy stopped in confusion. Falconer was at the head of the main alley leading into the Jews' domain before he missed Thomas. He turned and squinted in the boy's direction.

'Come. It is too cold to stand around. And before you ask, we are going to see your friend Hannah. She may be able to tell us something about the dead girl's book we have not asked before. Besides,' he added, after a short pause, 'I have something to collect.'

Falconer saw that Thomas was puzzled, but that he brightened up at the thought of seeing the young Jewess again. The boy wiped his nose on the edge of his cloak and hurried to keep up with the great strides of his Master. Falconer led a fast pace through the twists and turns of Jewry and Thomas hurried so that he did not get lost again. The wind was less in this warren of lanes, but looking up, Falconer could still see the scudding clouds, heavy and threatening above the rooftops. The day was well on now, and other people bustled about the lanes, their heavy robes bearing the two linen stripes that marked them as the 'King's property'. Curious glances were cast at the boy, but Falconer was known to the community, and he returned their friendly greetings in his best effort at the Hebrew tongue. It did not surprise Thomas that Master Falconer knew that arcane language, too.

It was Hannah who responded to Falconer's knock and a shy smile played across her lips as she invited them in. Apologizing for the absence of her father, who she said was attending to someone's needs, she led them to the back of the house and the comfortable room which led into the kitchen. It was where Thomas had first encountered her, apart from the embarrassment in the hallway.

'My father said you would call, and to give you this packet.'

Hannah handed a small cloth-bound bundle to Falconer, who took it gingerly, as though it were the most delicate jewellery. He could discern Thomas's curiosity, but he was not going to open the bundle in anyone's company. He was too embarrassed about its contents. Besides, other questions buzzed around his head like the bees in the chancellor's garden in summer. He could not resist posing them to Hannah.

'Margaret Gebetz. Would you have said she was a stupid girl?'

Hannah frowned, a little disconcerted by the suddenness of the question. Seeing her hesitate, Falconer rephrased it.

'Perhaps I should have said, was she a simple girl with a peasant education? After all, it is unusual for a girl of her background to be able to read.'

Hannah thought carefully before answering.

'You must understand we only met briefly each time, while Father prepared remedies for her master.'

'Even so.' Falconer's gaze seemed penetrating to Hannah, unaware of his poor sight. She licked her full lips nervously, and Falconer regretted his persistence. He smiled and, looking at Thomas who also seemed distraught by the pressure Hannah was under, said, 'I have worked young Thomas hard already today. I am sure that he could benefit from a morsel to keep his strength up.'

Hannah was clearly relieved to have something to do, and hurried into the kitchen to fetch bread and wine. Thomas was about to speak, when Falconer held up his hand.

'Don't worry, I will be gentle with your sweetheart.'

Thomas blushed and was about to stammer a denial, when Falconer hushed him with a finger to his lips. He strode across the room to the door leading on to the main hallway of the house. There were voices in conversation, one of which Falconer recognized as Samson's. He listened at the crack of the door as the herbalist explained a dosage to someone, his ears pricking up at the mention of bracken. The other person said he understood its usage. Someone whose fastidious tones Falconer thought he had discerned even as he spoke to Thomas. He inched open the door further and hissed for Thomas to come over.

'Who is that with Samson?'

Thomas applied his eye to the crack with curiosity.

'It's a Master – oldish, short hair, sharp nose. If you looked for yourself . . .'

Falconer interrupted. 'What is he doing?'

'He is taking a parcel. Just collecting a remedy,' offered Thomas, adding speculatively, 'as you have.'

'Perhaps,' said Falconer mysteriously. At that point Hannah returned with a simple bowl of bread and fruit, and Thomas was left wondering what Falconer saw in a seemingly ordinary event. Falconer motioned Thomas to eat and began again.

'Did Margaret say anything about her book when she gave it to you? Such as what it contained?'

'No. She just said to keep it safe as her life might depend on it.'

'Do you recall what it contained?'

'Not really, I didn't examine it after she had given it to me. And Thomas and I just glanced at it.'

Thomas nodded. 'It was just some scripture and a book of days.'

Falconer was a little disappointed. Although it was odd why Bonham had not mentioned the scriptures. Only the calendar. Hannah then corrected him on one point.

'And I've been thinking about what you said just now. Margaret couldn't read. She said that's why Master Fyssh trusted her with his messages. She even had to ask me once whose name was on a message.'

'Odd that she should own a book, then.'

'Oh, didn't I explain? It was not her book – she had taken it from the person she was scared of. She said while she had it, it would protect her.'

Hannah gazed sadly into Falconer's eyes. 'It didn't work, did it?'

Chapter Ten

Falconer was preparing himself for the banquet as well as he could. He took his best, indeed his only other, robe from the chest at the foot of his bed and spread it out. It was dull and green rather than black, and damp to his touch. He sighed – even the fur trim was moth-eaten. He spread it in front of the fire across his only chair and tried to draw some reasonable conclusions from the knowledge gained over the last few days, praying for guidance from Aristotle. Margaret Gebetz had been Fyssh's servant with little or no opportunity to steal a book from anyone else. Could he deduce that the book had been Fyssh's? Did it contain a secret, and was he therefore forced to kill her to keep her silent? Falconer was sure she had known her assailant. That fitted too. But if the murder of Moulcom was linked, why would Fyssh have committed that act, too? Unless Moulcom somehow knew of the first murder and had been using it against Fyssh. Perhaps that was why Moulcom had been at Beke's Inn that day. Both victims could have been killed because of some dangerous knowledge associated with the missing book. Now others had seen the book – would they be next? And was Fyssh the killer? Falconer hesitated.

'Forgive me, Aristotle. I am leaping to conclusions again.'

But what else fitted? There was something suspicious, too, about Bonham's behaviour, what with the bloody knife. And he had lied about the contents of the book. But Falconer did not have enough facts to promote him above Fyssh. Of course there was also de Stepyng. Falconer sighed. With him he had no more than a feeling. He might as well suspect the chancellor.

Clearly, he would have to keep an eye on everyone today. At least at the banquet they would all be under one roof. He hoped also that placing Thomas in the kitchens might pay off. Two pairs of eyes were better than one, especially when one pair couldn't see further than the end of his nose. That reminded him to ensure the parcel he had collected from Samson yesterday was safely stowed in his pouch. Then, turning to his steaming gown, he sighed and realized he would have to remain in his everyday garb.

John Fyssh had no such problems with his clothing. He indulged his desire for ostentation and had a chest bursting with robes of different hues. Clad only in his underlinen, he fingered various choices scattered across the bed. In the corner of the room, his knees pulled up and encircled by his arms sat the gloomy Hugh Pett. Fyssh grimaced at the boy.

'You are no longer a pleasure to me, child. Forever miserable, when there is so much to look forward to.'

Hugh could not imagine at this moment what pleasure there could be for him in the future and buried his head into his knees. He heard Fyssh approach him and felt the fat man's hand on his head, hot and sweaty. He decided then he must break away from his clutches, even if he had to reveal the depth of his sins to Master Falconer. Or kill the man himself. Fyssh put on a false, wheedling voice that Hugh had come to hate.

'Now tell me what you think I should wear. Should it be the red or the blue? Which most suits my complexion?'

Looking at the flushed face of the awful grotesque, Hugh was tempted to suggest he would blend perfectly with the red, but bit his tongue. Fyssh was capable of terrible rages and uncontrolled acts.

'Still silent, my pretty one? Well, I will deal with you some other time. I have more important matters to attend.'

He returned to the bed and picked up one of the undertunics. 'The blue I think, and the purple surcoat with the white borders.'

He eased his massive frame into the garments, pressing the folds down with his hands as though caressing his figure. He carefully arranged a sugar-loaf shaped hat on his head, covering his incipient baldness, and finally belted a pouch around his ample waist. He primped himself before Hugh.

'Tell me how I look.'

Huge gave no reply, so Fyssh grasped his chin in his fat fingers, squeezing his lips together in the parody of a pout.

'Perhaps I will keep you. You are at least prettier than that horrid Northerner, Moulcom.'

Fyssh shuddered at the thought.

'I was much cheered by his death. He came here throwing his weight around in search of that book everyone seems interested in. Well, now I know why and who should be worried about its existence.'

'But the book is burned. Thomas said Master Bonham had burned it.'

'Ah, you do still have a tongue. I do not know what your little friend was told, but it was a lie. I should know.'

He patted the pouch that hung at his waist.

'And what I know will be of enormous value to me.'

As Thomas turned the spit, the heat of the fire roasting him almost as much as the haunch of meat, he reflected that he had not come far from his parents' farm after all. His vision of academic Oxford was now limited to the chancellor's kitchen. The stone arch under which Thomas sat was carved with an array of devilish beasts, hanging as though in flight. Leathery wings and wild grimaces out of which poked serpents' tongues menaced the unfortunate turnspit. The association of demons and the fire below was clearly a perpetual warning against straying from the straight and narrow. The ceiling was high to accommodate the heat and smoke, such that the upper part of the room, trussed with oak beams, was barely visible through the haze. The floor was of worn red bricks, stained with many ancient culinary accidents. Huge copper pots hung from the walls, along with a bewildering collection of strainers, graters and other devices whose use Thomas could not fathom. Across the great oaken table dominating the middle of the room was an army of knives, and a scarred wooden chopping block on which the cook was hacking a side of beef into small pieces. His huge hands raked the knife across the flesh, and images of Margaret Gebetz's slit throat were conjured up in Thomas's mind. Numerous other skivvies scurried hither and thither between pantry and scullery, buttery and larder. The cook marshalled his assistants, many of them poor students like Thomas, as though he were a king on a battlefield. Which in a way he was, for his position as master cook was revered generally, and the preparation of a successful meal required careful strategy. Victory could only be ensured with a careful deployment of resources.

Even though it had been Falconer's idea for him to work at the banquet, Thomas was grateful for the meal he would earn doing so. He gazed in awe as the cook dumped handfuls of the chopped beef into a cauldron hung over the fire. He followed that up with an array of spices such as Thomas had never seen before. The cook intoned their names like some secret incantation as he put them in.

'Ginger, cubebs, cloves, mace, cinnamon, sage and parsley.'

He plunged his hand into the already hot water and stirred all the ingredients together, muttering his pleasure. All would not be ready however, until the meat had stewed to a manageable mush, and further quantities of saffron, salt and vinegar had been added. The cook's art would not be satisfied until it was impossible for the eater to know the meat amidst the host of flavours.

Falconer had been instrumental in getting Thomas into the kitchen preparing the banquet for Prince Edward for a specific purpose. Having been alerted along with the other regent masters of arts of the requirement to attend, he saw an opportunity to observe his principal suspects in the matter of the two murders. It was Thomas's commission to keep an eye on things from the kitchen, and as a server of the food. When he asked Falconer what he was looking for, his reply was, as usual, enigmatic.

'I do not know, but you will when you see it.'

It was another voice that brought Thomas back to the present – the harsher voice of the cook.

'If you do not even have the brain to turn a spit properly, I do not think you will make a good student.'

Thomas muttered an apology and began again to turn the meat he had neglected in his daydream. He would have to do better to carry out Falconer's wishes. As the cook returned to stir his stew, he asked him what the other, small pot was for.

'Why the sauce, of course. It's a pity there is no swan available as I know a good sauce to be made from its liver, heart and blood.'

There was a look of true regret on his red, perspiring face.

His melancholy was interrupted by someone calling his name, and he turned towards the door. Hidden behind the cook's generous frame, Thomas could not see who it was who had come to the kitchen until the cook turned away with a small packet in his hand. Then he saw Joshua's profile as the Jew turned to leave. There was a livid purple bruise down the side of his face. Clearly he had survived the fall from the tower, and not in some superhuman way. The bruises showed he was as fragile as any Christian.

'I also need more bay,' called the cook.

Joshua turned his head back and looked into the kitchen, nodding. Thomas bowed his head, and was not sure whether Joshua had seen him or not.

'At last,' said the cook as he returned to the table with the packet. 'I had run out of saffron.'

Restored to good humour, he then proceeded with great crushing thrusts to pound a pile of almonds in his mortar into a pulp.

It was already after sext and as Falconer made his way through the streets to the King's hall, there were other regent masters hurrying to the feast. Falconer's poor sight often gave others the impression that he was aloof. It was not so, he merely could not recognize faces until they were very close and was embarrassed to admit it. De Stepyng had no reservations about accosting him, however. He saw the large, slightly stooped figure ahead of him wearing everyday garb, and instantly recognized it as Falconer. He hurried to catch him up, having to put his hand on the other man's sleeve before he acknowledged him. Why was Falconer so reticent, especially when it was necessary to find something out? He tried to fall in step with the other's strides and found himself hurrying.

'Falconer, do you know which side the slippery Edward is on for the moment?'

'I am as ignorant of the court as the simplest peasant. Why ask me?'

De Stepyng's breath came in harsh gasps as he rushed along beside Falconer. He was well beyond his fiftieth year.

'It is important for all of us to know which side we are on, when the country is at war with itself,' he lectured. 'I myself am clearly with the barons in this matter. It is the only way to rid the country of Henry's French clique who pervert his mind and bankrupt the nation.'

'Yet Henry is still our king.'

De Stepyng's anger was rising, yet it seemed an overreaction to Falconer.

'I know what these idle hangers-on can do. They are so seductive. I have half a mind to refuse to eat with the prince, if he has returned to his father's cause.'

'The chancellor is for the barons' cause, but can still eat with the son of the King of England. Myself, I'm just looking forward to some good food.'

Falconer's flippancy seemed to put de Stepyng off and he strode beside him silently for a while. The ground was muddy and churned by the many feet making their way through the streets. Ahead in the growing crowd, de Stepyng saw Fyssh stepping fussily over puddles, and watched with curiosity as the fat man pulled a book from his purse and examined it as though for reassurance. He spoke curtly to Falconer.

'The servant girl.'

Falconer turned his head questioningly.

'Fyssh's servant girl – did you assuage your curiosity about her death?'

The crowd got heavier as they passed through the narrow

arch of Smith Gate. No king, or future monarch, set foot inside the walls of Oxford as there was a tradition that no good would come to one who did. King's hall, in all its sumptuousness, was located beyond the walls. The crowd reminded Falconer again of a flock of crows squabbling over a corpse. Though now many had exchanged their sober, everyday clothes for more colourful attire. From their chatter, perhaps starlings were a more apt comparison. On the steps leading into the hall the two regent masters stood momentarily still as others jostled for a better place.

'Aristotle has not yet shown me the answer, but the facts begin to indicate a probable person.'

De Stepyng did not wait to hear whether Falconer would reveal whom he suspected. He offered his own opinion.

'The man you want is ahead of us. Fyssh killed his own servant.'

'Why would he do that?'

'Because she knew.'

'Knew? Knew what?'

The regent masters were now pushing each other like unruly students in their haste to be nearest the top table. De Stepyng was elbowed away from Falconer, but his final words were audible in the babel.

'Of his ways with boys. Murder must be a minor step for a sodomist.'

That gave Falconer pause for thought, and he stood in the archway of the great hall fitting the new fact into his collection of truths. Abruptly he was reminded of where he was when those behind him began to push him in the small of his back, complaining at his large frame blocking the doorway. He turned to glare at the nearest man, small and pale-faced, and the voices around him immediately subsided. These were, after all, thinkers, not men of action. Falconer, with his chequered past, was more robust than most of the Masters, and they knew it. He turned back and ahead of him could just make out de Stepyng's progress being stopped by Fyssh. Even with his poor eyesight, Falconer could tell it was him from the purple surcoat, which stood out from all others. Whether something was said or not, de Stepyng pulled away angrily. Then Falconer lost both in the crowd.

The hall was high with dark, heavy wooden buttresses supporting the roof arch. Banners hung from the walls, somewhat faded but discernible as royal. There were gaps where coats of arms of certain barons had been discreetly removed. Down the two long walls ran sturdy trestle tables with benches either side of them. The floor between the tables was freshly strewn with rushes and in the centre of the hall a good fire already blazed sending smoke plumes up to the louvre in the roof. Servants already scurried back and forth between the tables, and regent masters settled themselves in favoured places. Some, overly concerned with their social status, sat close to the dais at the far end of the room to be near the prince. Others, more practical, occupied places in the centre of the hall close to the fire.

Sufficient daylight filtered through the high, glazed windows not to require cressets in the body of the hall. However, candles blazed extravagantly on the white damask of the table set for the prince and chancellor on the dais. A single gold plate was set for the prince, with simpler items for the others on the high table. Perhaps the chancellor still did not wish to entirely commit himself and the university to the prince. Or did not wish to show how rich he was to avoid too high a contribution to the prince's funds. However, there was one clear acknowledgement of the importance of the guest at the feast. The centre of the table was adorned with a nef in the form of a silver ship in full sail, its high prow and stern housing a salt-cellar, towels, and knives and spoons for the prince's use. Falconer knew this ornament only came out on great occasions, and was de Cantilupe's acknowledgement of Prince Edward's future importance to his own career. The chancellorship of the whole of England was not beyond his grasp after all.

It was now vital for Falconer to be able to see what his main suspects were doing. Around him, the seated figures merged into a sea of dark robes spotted with pink blurs that were their faces. It was hopeless – he could not distinguish the person a few feet away let alone anyone at the other end of the hall. He fumbled in the pouch at his waist and withdrew the cloth-wrapped bundle Hannah had given him. Carefully unwrapping the parcel, he extracted a device that old Samson had made specially for him. The light angling in through the high windows above him sparkled on two crystal circles embedded in metal. Each circle was at one end of a v-shape also made in metal. Falconer self-consciously held the point of the v against his forehead with the circles of glass over each eye. The hall and its occupants swam into remarkable focus. He realized that if he looked out of the corner of his eye, the straight edge of the table curved to the same degree as the lens. However, by steadfastly gazing forward and turning his head, Falconer was able to see as clearly as he had as a boy.

His companions either side gave him a curious glance but everyone else seemed busy talking to their neighbour. The noise was worse than that coming from a bunch of unruly students awaiting a lecture. Falconer swivelled on his bench and saw that Bonham was at the table on the opposite side of the hall facing him. He was already deep in conversation with the person to his right, who, by the look on his face, was being treated to a typically pedantic lecture from the little man. Falconer was glad he was not trapped next to him. Nearer the high table, but with his back to Falconer, sat Fyssh, his rich surcoat standing out in the sea of more sober garb. His fat backside spilled copiously over the bench.

At first Falconer could not find de Stepyng. Then he leaned forward across the table and looked hard to his right. He discerned the hawk nose of de Stepyng only three or four places away from him. He was staring sourly into space. The main protagonists were in place – would their behaviour reveal anything of value? Falconer had been optimistic with young Thomas, but had to admit to himself that he was entirely unsure what he expected to happen. He simply needed more facts, however trivial they may seem on their own. Friar Bacon would have reminded him of the need for scientific observation in all matters.

He became aware of the increasingly curious gaze of the Master sitting to his right, and realized he still sat with one fist held to his forehead and the odd device over his eyes. Reluctantly he returned to the world of blurred vision, dropping the lenses into his lap for immediate retrieval. He treated the offending Master to one of his unnerving glares; the Master coughed nervously and deliberately began a conversation with an elderly regent master sitting on the opposite side to Falconer.

A blaring trumpet in the gallery above everyone's head proclaimed the arrival of the guest of honour.

Chapter Eleven

Prince Edward presented a robust figure as he strode on to the dais followed by the chancellor. His long legs, clad in shining decorative greaves, carried him easily to the table. His upper body was draped with a blue tabard emblazoned with three yellow lions. He stopped beside the ornate chair at the centre of the high table, and scanned the gathered throng of Masters. His drooping left eyelid somehow conveyed an air of friendly complicity. Turning to put a powerful arm on the chancellor's shoulder, it was clear he was a head taller than de Cantilupe. A circlet topped his long raven locks – he was every inch a leader of men.

The tense silence in the hall was broken by a quiet laugh from Edward's lips. That and the words he spoke to the chancellor, causing him to smile, gave every indication that he and the university were in accord. He dropped gracefully into his seat and a ripple ran down the hall as regent masters breathed out in relief and sat down. Falconer quickly raised the device to his eyes and scanned the crowd again. Everyone was still in place and he relaxed a little. He could not help but be impressed by Edward, and could understand how his plausible nature would win men over. How different he seemed from his apparently weak and easily led father, the King. Even his physical size was greater than Henry's, though they shared the same oddity of a drooping eyelid. With the lenses held to his eyes, he surveyed the prince as he leaned across and spoke to de Cantilupe. They were clearly two men of power who had found something to share.

As Edward leaned back in his chair, the chancellor waved his hand and the ceremony of the feast began. One of the kitchen staff came forward and tasted the bread and salt laid out on the high table. Next a youth with a great pitcher of water came forward – Falconer knew this too would have been tasted to avoid suspicion of poison. Edward washed his hands and dried them on a towel. He was followed in this ceremony by the chancellor, and more perfunctorily by everyone down the hall, served by young students. Falconer was nudged from behind by the server bringing his water, and turned to reprimand the clumsy individual. The mischievous face of Thomas Symon confronted him.

'Keep your eyes on the others,' Falconer hissed. 'I am not under suspicion here.'

Blushing, Thomas hurried away to the kitchens to assist in serving the food, and Falconer smiled at his discomfiture.

Back in the kitchen, the cook fussed lining up the students who were his servitors at the feast and passing them the dishes on which lay the first course. Glassy-eyed pike swam before Thomas's gaze as the platters of fish were passed out. As he stood at the back of the line, he was entrusted with the other part of the first course. This was some indistinguishable dark-skinned fowl, which nevertheless smelled so aromatic as to make Thomas's mouth water. Along the line of food-laden boys scurried an old man dressed up in a stiff blue robe and waving a thin wand. He reviewed the ranks as though they were troops, then stood at their head and nodded to the cook. Halegod had taken the role of steward for his own, revelling in the ceremony and attention. The cook peered round the kitchen doors and a second flurry of trumpeting sounded out in the main hall. The meal was to begin.

Thomas saw that he could keep an eye on both Bonham and Fyssh if he stationed himself at the top of the long table opposite Falconer. Another youth was making his way there, so Thomas bustled past him, almost tipping over the other's tray of food. Startled, the youth began to shout a protest, but the stern gaze of Halegod, who had missed Thomas's manoeuvre, stopped him. Thomas began to serve the dark meat which had already been sliced in the kitchen. Serving from the middle of the hall, he had to lean over the table to put food on the trenchers of those who sat facing him. Gradually he worked his way towards Fyssh who sat with his back to Thomas. Leaning over his shoulder, he strove to hear what Fyssh might be saying to his neighbour and was disappointed to hear him denigrating the chancellor's supply of wine.

'Of course, the man keeps the best wines for himself – good French wines from Poitou and Guienne – and serves us concoctions manufactured by his butler. Then he has the nerve to call himself an ascetic. Him and his hair shirt indeed.'

Thomas moved quickly on to Bonham, who faced him across the table. He served him the last slivers of the fowl, and stared at him as though he could shame the man into a public con-fession of murder. Thomas was still convinced of his guilt. Bonham merely stared blankly back, as though he did not recall that Thomas was the youth from whom he had taken the all-important book.

From the other side of the hall, Falconer could just discern that Thomas was moving close to his quarry. He raised the lenses to his eyes in time to see the boy staring brazenly at Bonham. That was not what he had told him to do. Had he not said that he wanted Thomas to observe discreetly? Nor was he watching what he was doing with his heavy serving plate of duck. Falconer watched in exasperation as Thomas became the centre of attention by tipping the last remnants off his plate all over the Master sitting opposite Bonham. There was an uproar, studiously ignored by the high table, and Halegod arrived to whip Thomas back into the kitchen.

'You are the clumsiest oaf I have ever come across,' railed the old man. 'You will stay in the kitchen and assist the cook.'

Thomas began to protest, but Halegod stopped him with a raised palm.

'Just imagine what would have happened if you had tipped food over the prince.'

As he stalked off, Thomas realized he had indeed been so absorbed in his errand for Falconer that he had forgotten to sneak a look at Prince Edward. He had been a few feet away from the man who should become King of England and had not seen him. He had also ruined his chance of observing his Master's suspects in the murder hunt. He sank on his haunches by the fire and stared gloomily into the flames.

Falconer too was consumed by gloom. So far nothing had happened that might confirm the murderer's identity for him. The first course was complete, and Falconer's only observation was that de Stepyng had picked at both fish and fowl, seeming ill at ease. Between the first and second courses the cook had occasioned audible approval by serving a subtlety – several sugary representations of swans which hardly survived the expression of approval before they were torn apart by sweet-toothed regent masters. Only Thomas would have known they were second best for the cook, who had mourned not being able to prepare the real bird. The next course was now being served – an aromatic stew, ladled thick and hot on to new trenchers.

As a boy came to serve de Stepyng, who was noticeably more agitated as time progressed, the sallow-faced Master arose from his seat, almost knocking the ladle from the servitor's hand. There was a momentary silence into which de Stepyng's voice cut sharply.

'I cannot share meat with the child of a tyrant, who himself supports tyranny.'

The words were spoken pointedly to the high table, then de Stepyng turned and coolly walked out of the great hall, a sea of shocked faces following him. The silence was broken by the prince.

'Earl Simon is welcome to those with poor digestion, and poor judgement.'

The laughter following that remark was not all natural. Many faces bore fixed smiles, for many at the university tacitly supported the baronial cause. The time would come when sides would have to be openly chosen. For the time being, the prospect of further good food soon reinstated the spirit of the event.

Meanwhile, Thomas was busy scrubbing dirty pans with sand to scour them clean. The vast stone sinks were off the main kitchen area, and so he was hidden from sight when Joshua returned to bring the cook more culinary herbs and spices. He was, however, in a position to see and hear most of what happened in the kitchen. The cook at first raged at the young Jew for returning so late and snatched the bunch of leaves from him, hurling them to the floor.

'Too late,' he roared. 'It is the ginger I require.'

He had already boiled and sieved the pears, mixed them with

sugar, honey and cinnamon and boiled the mixture again. To the cooled concoction he had added numerous yolks of egg. The thickened pudding now required a sprinkling of powdered ginger, for they were almost ready for it in the hall. Servitors scurried back and forth with dirty salvers and pots from the meat course. They clattered the pots into Thomas's sink, and most of the cook's castigation of Joshua was drowned out. The Jew seemed unconcerned by the criticism, grinning and chewing methodically on something he took from the pouch at his waist. He tossed a pot into the grasp of the fat cook and watched him as the man hurried across the kitchen to see to his pudding. As Joshua passed the archway beyond which stood Thomas, he fumbled in his pouch again and produced a leaf, at the same time carelessly dropping a couple on the floor. He stuffed the leaf into his mouth and stared straight at Thomas. The boy was petrified until he realized there was a blankness in the Jew's gaze. Seeming to be unaware of his adversary, Joshua turned away, chewing on his leaf.

Thomas put down the pan he had been scouring and stepped forward into the archway.

'Boy. Help me with this dish.'

The cook was already doling the charewarden pudding into shallow bowls.

'And try not to spill it all over me. I will not be as forbearing as that regent master you drowned.'

Starting forward, Thomas automatically stooped and picked up the leaves that Joshua had dropped, thrusting them into his pouch.

Once the pudding was consumed, the hubbub of voices in the hall increased as the naturally argumentative Masters embarked on discourses with their fellows. Falconer's neighbour at table drew him into a disputation about the efficacy of blood-letting. Debating the merits of leeches, Falconer realized he was not concentrating on the more urgent matter in hand. He once more surveyed the hall. Fyssh and Bonham were still in place, and he relaxed again. There was a momentary respectful silence as Edward and de Cantilupe rose and left the hall, deep in conversation. Then the hubbub began again and Falconer realized his neighbour was talking to him.

'As for myself, I believe cupping to be more specific than the application of leeches.'

'And yet,' rejoined Falconer, as though he had heard and weighed every word his neighbour had spoken. 'The blood seems to clot more swiftly after removal of the leech. Have you not observed this?'

Having thought that Falconer was inattentive or ignorant of medical matters, the man was lost for words at this most acute of observations. Falconer took the opportunity to raise his lenses to his eyes and scan the hall more carefully. Just in time, he saw Fyssh rise and make his way towards Bonham, leaning over the table to address him. He whispered a few words in the little man's ear and Bonham's face paled in shock. He half-turned towards Fyssh and nodded his head curtly. His bloated face creased with a broad smile, Fyssh waddled past the table and disappeared under an arch in the far corner of the room. He was making for the kitchen area, and Falconer hoped that Thomas was alert. Returning the scrutiny of his lenses to Bonham, Falconer fancied he could see a worried man. What had Fyssh said to him that had resulted in such a grim visage? Bonham's head drooped over the table momentarily, then as he looked up his eyes locked with Falconer's. He dropped his lenses and turned again to the eager blood-letter at his side.

'Tell me, do you also believe that the last Monday in April is a dangerous day for blood-letting?'

In the kitchen there was a cacophony of noise, too. It did not, however, match the erudite discourse of the Masters in the hall. Everyone was relieved that the feast had gone well, and pots and utensils were piled, temporarily forgotten in the vast sinks. The kitchen servants and poor students mingled together laughing over incidents such as Thomas spilling food all over Regent Master Feakes. His fellow students thought it a great treat, and the cook was now inclined to view it with more amusement. Sprawled beside the fire his great red face glowed no less powerfully than the flames themselves. He stoked his inner glow with long draughts of red wine straight from the heavy flask clutched in his beefy hand.

Thomas sat nervously on the edge of the group of happy individuals, wondering if there was anything he should be doing to assist Falconer. He had not been much use to date, and didn't know what Falconer was looking for. Or even if he knew who the murderer loose in Oxford was. It all seemed so confusing, and the Master's determined logical deductions did not make sense to Thomas. Falconer seemed to be favouring Fyssh as the killer, yet Thomas's instincts led him straight toward Bonham. Or Joshua the Jew. Thinking of Joshua reminded him of the leaves the youth had dropped on the kitchen floor. They were no doubt some culinary herb, yet all sorts of odd items appeared to hold great significance for Master Falconer. He pulled the two leaves out of his pouch and examined them. They seemed ordinary and smelled of nothing, hardly suitable as a culinary herb. Nothing made sense to him, yet Master Falconer seemed to know exactly what he was doing.

*　　　*　　　*

Falconer was not sure what to do next. Distracted by a stupid desire to show up the ignorance of his neighbour at the table, he had missed Bonham leaving his place. Now both Fyssh and Bonham were God knows where, and de Stepyng had left long ago. How was he to fill the gap in his deductive logic when everyone was out of his sight? He had thought to test each one after the feast when they should have been at their most relaxed. Now there was no one to talk to. He might as well see whether Thomas had discovered anything in his clumsy eavesdropping.

No one paid any attention as he slipped through the archway into the kitchen area in search of his young assistant. He found him sitting on the edge of a happy group of youths, all being regaled with stories of culinary disaster by the rotund and obviously drunken cook.

'. . . And he ate the stew, feathers and all.'

The story brought forth peals of laughter, and Falconer smiled and sank down beside Thomas.

'Have you seen anyone come this way?'

Thomas shook his head, then changed his mind.

'Well, only Joshua. He dropped these.'

Falconer took one of the leaves from the boy and sniffed it.

'But I don't suppose it's important. I mean, they couldn't be poisonous because he was eating them.'

Out of curiosity, Falconer popped the leaf into his mouth and tentatively chewed. It seemed pleasant. Still, Joshua did not figure on his mental list of candidates. He needed to find Fyssh or Bonham – de Stepyng need not be considered for the moment. Chewing absently on the leaf, he began to feel strangely relaxed despite his worries. He grinned inanely at the cook and tried to recall why he had come into the kitchen. Another poor student was telling a story, and although Falconer could not hear it properly, he felt inclined to laugh uproariously at the end of it. Someone sitting next to him turned and gave him a curious look. Didn't the fool understand he was enjoying himself? The cook spat into the fire and the flames crackled and seem to curl out towards Falconer. He rocked back and clutched at the side of the open hearth. The stone felt curiously soft, warm and scaly. The carved gargoyle under his hand seemed to shift, sending a cold shudder through him. Surely it was just the flickering of the flames that moved the shadows of the carving? Several pairs of eyes now turned in his direction, and he backed away from their menacing glare into the shadows of the arch leading to the scullery. He pressed his face against the cold stone and calmed himself.

It was lucky that he had moved because from where he was he could look over the people grouped around the fire, and in that moment saw a fat figure pass the open kitchen door. Surely that was Fyssh – why was he still lurking around? Falconer began to concentrate again on his reason for being here, and crossed the kitchen to follow the suspected Master.

Thomas got up as he saw Falconer pass him. But the Master firmly pressed him back on to his seat, and uncharacteristically winked at him.

'Stay here,' he whispered with a conspiratorial smile.

The cook and his gang ignored him as he skirted the table, scattered with the debris of the recent repast, and continued swapping tales. Reaching the door, he peered cautiously round its edge in the direction Fyssh had been going. The vast figure was at the end of the passage, turning towards the cellars under the hall. A torch at the end of the passage cast his shadow back even larger than life along the wall. It seemed to leap towards Falconer and he flinched momentarily. Then Fyssh was down the steps and his shadow was gone. The corridor rocked gently as though Falconer were in a small boat fishing off the coast.

He braced his legs apart and scurried after Fyssh. Turning towards the doorway down to the cellars, he thought he saw the glow of flames, and smelled an evil odour. Was Fyssh in league with the Devil? He hesitated at the arch, leaning on a frame that creaked and bowed, then cautiously descended the steps, keeping in close contact with the wall to his left. At the bottom he could just see the shape of Fyssh under an arch to his right. The man was leaning on a barrel of similar proportions to himself, seemingly doing nothing. If he had conjured up the Devil, he had not arrived yet.

Falconer needed to get nearer, but could not cross the floor of the cellar directly towards Fyssh. He would be seen instantly, even by the weak light of the brazier on the wall. Edging around the wall, he moved behind a stack of barrels in a direction that would bring him out behind the waiting man. As he slid between the barrels and the wall, he heard a rustling sound from amidst the pile. Part of his mind told him it was rats, but then he thought he heard his own name being called.

'William.'

The sound seemed to boom around the chamber and Falconer's mouth went dry as he recognized the voice of his father, long dead. He spat the chewed leaf out on the ground, shivering. Then just as suddenly the sound was gone. Recovering control, he peered over the top of the barrels expecting Fyssh to have been alerted by the noise and to have fled. Nothing had happened – Fyssh still leaned against the barrel, tapping the surface impatiently. He seemed oblivious to all the clamour that Falconer had heard. Not able to believe his luck, Falconer gave thanks that he was still undiscovered. He was still not as close as he had wanted to be, but before he could move again Fyssh turned and spoke to someone in the shadows of the archway. His voice was muffled by the low ceiling and Falconer could not make out what he said. Whoever else was in the cellar was not revealing himself, because Fyssh was peering with surprise into the dark. The fat man produced something from the pouch at his ample waist and waved it in front of him. Falconer edged round the pile of barrels to get a better view of who it was facing Fyssh but he was hidden.

He did get a glimpse of a dark sleeve as the other's arm clutched at whatever it was Fyssh was holding out. The echoes of their argument boomed around the cellar, turning the words into an incomprehensible mad cacophony. Gusts of air blew the flames of the brazier into wild disorder. Falconer could see the shadows of demons flying across the arched roof. At the centre of this mad scene two men struggled, seemingly locked as one around the object both craved. There was a flash of light and Fyssh's head arched back in an impossible position. Rivers of blood flew towards Falconer and his nerve cracked. He screamed and fled from what could be no less than the Apocalypse. Turning to look back, he saw a great bat flying towards him, its wings cracking with the effort. He stumbled up the steps, and swung around the doorway, tearing his hand on the rough wood. The sanctuary of the kitchen was just at the end of the corridor, and he could still hear the sound of voices – human voices. A claw grabbed at his heel, just as he forced himself to move again. He staggered forward and fell on his face. He could feel the hot breath of the demon on his neck. He screwed himself into a ball and screamed as loud as he could. The sound seemed to come from the depths of his soul, and echoed around his skull. Once started he could not stop it.

The cook was the first on the scene, and later swore that there had been no one but Falconer in the passageway. Thomas had had to break through the knot of kitchen servants in front of him, and had feared the worst when he saw Falconer on the floor covered in blood. However the cook was already turning him over, and he could see Falconer's chest heaving with the effort of his screams. The blood came from a nasty gash in his hand, but that would mend. At first Falconer thrashed in the firm grasp of the cook's beefy hands. But when Thomas repeatedly called his name, he began to calm.

'Thomas, is that you?'

'You will know if you open your eyes, Master.'

Falconer tentatively raised his eyelids, and looked all around.

'The demon. Is he gone?'

As soon as he said the words he felt foolish. But what was it he had seen, then? The cook helped him to his feet, and looking over his shoulder he was sure he saw a red glow emanating from the cellar. He began to shake again, but the strange feelings were receding.

'Who were you following?'

Thomas's question brought him back to reality.

'Master Fyssh.'

His response brought back something of the strange vision he had seen.

'He's still in the cellar.'

Falconer knew he would have to face the descent again. Still unsure of what was real, and whether or not the Devil lurked below, he insisted no one should follow him. Neither the cook nor Thomas chose to argue. He went to the doorway leading to the cellar, noticing the rusty latch covered in blood where he must have cut himself. The cellar was poorly lit by a guttering brazier, and Falconer with his poor eyes had to venture further to verify if Fyssh were still present. A cold breeze blew from the other end of the cellar, causing what little light there was to dance across a heap of clothes on the floor. Falconer bent over it. Not a heap of clothes but the body of Master Fyssh. His head lay at a curious angle, his eyes staring blankly into the depths of the cellar. His heavy chins could not conceal the livid gash that had nearly decapitated him. He lay in his own blood, the purple surcoat soaking it up. One of Falconer's murder suspects lay dead, apparently killed in the same way as the servant girl whose death had started this chain of events.

Falconer drew out the new device to focus his vision, relieved that his combat with the Devil had not broken it. With it he scanned the body more carefully before anyone else could disturb it. One of Fyssh's arms was raised above his head, as though he had been protecting something. Falconer examined the claw of his fist more closely. There was some parchment – a letter perhaps – in his grasp. Falconer prised the fingers open and found the cover and first few pages of a small book. As he rose, he thought there was someone observing him deeper in the recesses of the cellar. Forgetting his eye-lenses he started forward, peering into the gloom. There was a grey shape, but it had turned and gone before Falconer raised the device to his eyes. Hearing a crash, he ran forward into the dark, only to find another flight of steps leading up to a trap-door. It was closed and must have been the origin of the noise. Whoever, or whatever had been in the cellar was now gone.

'Is it safe down there, Master?'

The distant voice of the cook called from the top of the steps. Hurriedly Falconer slipped the torn cover into his pouch and returned to the body.

'I fear that Master Fyssh will give no more lectures. You had better summon the authorities.'

Chapter Twelve

Falconer woke with a start, a feathery memory at the back of his mind of a scaly lizard crawling over him, its thin tongue flicking across his eyelids. The room was empty and brightly lit by the sun streaming through the casement. Dust motes danced in the beams of light, which shone directly on the pallet opposite. He was back in his own room in Aristotle's hall, and it took him a little while to recall the events of the previous day. At least it took a while to remember them in a sensible way. He gently lowered his legs on to the straw-covered floor and tried to get up. After a moment of lightheadedness, when he thought he might float out of the window, he grew steady and made for the door. He could hear voices in the main hall, and made his way towards them. One was clearly that of Thomas Symon, whose aggrieved tones were admonishing some fellow student. On opening the door, he saw Thomas, and an ashen Hugh Pett sitting opposite each other across the stained and pitted table used for meals.

'Ahh. I know I am a little late, but have we anything to eat?'

Hugh rose and barged past Falconer out of the hall, his face a mask.

'What did I say?' Falconer turned to Thomas in puzzlement. The boy reminded him that, after they had returned to the hall last night, Hugh had seen Falconer in his room, and emerged white-faced and silent. He had refused to tell Thomas what had passed between him and Falconer.

'And I surely can't remember,' said Falconer, searching his still muddled memories of the previous day. Then he dismissed it from his mind.

'You youngsters believe the world and all its happenings revolve around you. When in reality we are all no more than a mote in God's eye.'

He reached out for a stale crust left on the table, and tried to rationalize the main events in King's hall. He thought aloud.

'Going into the hall, Fyssh argued with de Stepyng. After the meal he said something unpleasant to Bonham to judge by his reaction. All had left the hall by the time I met you in the kitchen. As had the chancellor, of course, with Prince Edward.'

'You do not think that he—'

Thomas's vivid imagination was held in check by a firm look from Falconer.

'No. I believe we can rule out our noble prince.'

He sighed.

'As we can now Master Fyssh.'

'Could he not still be our killer? If indeed the Devil took him, that may be conclusive proof of his guilt.'

'I fear it was a more human hand that dispatched our fat friend. And a murderer himself murdered may be convenient, but is not logical in the circumstances. No, there is much more to uncover here before the final truth. Just when I thought I needed one more truth to deduce the greater one, I am presented with another skein of truths unwinding that lead me further from the path.'

Thomas stirred uncomfortably in his seat.

'But you insisted you had seen the Devil when we found you yesterday.'

Falconer blushed in embarrassment.

'I wish you could forget that. Oh, I do believe in the existence of the Devil. But not in a cellar in Oxford, meeting a rather overweight and overrated regent master.'

'But then, what did you see?'

'Quite simply, I saw Fyssh's murderer. And probably the murderer of Margaret Gebetz and Jack Moulcom. A pity I was in no fit state to recognize him.'

Thomas was confused.

By way of an explanation, Falconer asked for another of the leaves Joshua had dropped in the kitchen. Taking it from Thomas's fingers, he raised it to his nostrils.

'For a herb it is remarkably short of aroma. As a drug, it was very potent.'

He put it to his lips, then, recalling the Apocalyptic images his mind had woven the previous day, he stopped and stowed it carefully in his pouch.

'I know who can help us identify this. Come.'

Peter Bullock was trying hard to be patient with the young student before him. He had stepped out of his door that cold morning, to find this boy standing shivering in the shadow of the Great Keep. He had sought to ignore him, turning left to go about his business, but the youth had stepped across his path. He clearly was not going to be ignored, and Bullock sighed, his breath expelling in a frosty cloud.

'Well?'

The youth hesitated, dropping his head so that his fine red hair masked his face. He mumbled something that Bullock's imperfect hearing could not catch. Impatiently, he grunted a query.

'I killed Master Fyssh,' the boy blurted, a look of anguish on his thin face.

'That is a university matter. Go and see the chancellor or the proctors.'

Once again Bullock moved to pass the boy, but again he was stopped by the quick movement of the student. Hugh Pett did not know why he had sought out the constable rather than the university authorities in order to make his confession. He only knew that Master Falconer would not listen to him, and had no one else to confide in but this ugly and bodily twisted man.

'They will not believe me.'

'And I will?'

Hugh's eyes implored his attention, and Bullock relented.

'You had better come inside. You look as though you have spent the whole night in the gutter outside my house.'

Inside he had offered the boy some ale warmed over the coals in his firegrate. Then he had gently coaxed him into telling him what he had meant about killing the regent master at yesterday's feast. At first Hugh would only repeat that he had wished Fyssh dead, and had made it happen. Now Bullock was curious and wanted more. He began to press for more details.

'Where did you get this?' Samson's tone was peremptory as he gazed at Thomas through his red-tinged lenses with piercing eyes. He was twirling the leaf that Falconer had given him in his delicate fingers. The intertwining scents that pervaded Samson's house made Thomas feel dizzy. Or perhaps it was the presence of the Jew's daughter Hannah, sitting demurely and discreetly in the corner of the room. Thomas took a deep breath to clear his head and spoke.

'From Joshua.'

'Joshua?'

Samson's tone was disbelieving.

'Well, indirectly. He dropped some leaves on the floor and

I . . . picked them up. I saw him eating them and thought they were just herbs.'

Falconer interrupted.

'It tasted nice when I chewed one.'

'Oh, it does. Or at least, you feel nice. Mostly.'

'So you know what this leaf is?'

'I do. It is known to the Arabs as khat.'

Samson explained that the leaf grew in the Land of Ham, in Ethiop. There it was used socially by the Mohammedans who eschewed ale and wines. It relaxed and gave a feeling of calm, but it had other paradoxical effects. Some people who ate it were known to go mad temporarily and claim everyone hated them. Some people imagined persecutions, living in a waking nightmare. Falconer thought he could vouch for that. Samson continued, 'Fortunately, they come round and are not harmed. Unless they do something to themselves or others while in that state.'

'And Joshua has this leaf? Why do you allow it?'

Samson turned his weary gaze to Hannah. She nodded at her father. 'They deserve an explanation.'

'Take them to Rabbi Jehozadok, he will explain better than I. He is the youth's guardian. Give him the leaf by way of explanation.'

Bullock's interrogation of Hugh Pett was progressing well, although the information the boy had given to date could have been got from word of mouth circulating in the street. If the boy truly did kill Fyssh, he needed more information to present to the chancellor. Perhaps he could test what he knew on his friend Falconer first. Pett knew that the murder had occurred in the cellar of the great dining hall, and that it had been committed with a knife. He clearly hated Fyssh for some reason

– reason enough to kill him, obviously. And he had confessed, after all.

'Come,' he grated harshly, and the boy jerked up his head that had been cast down at the ground.

'What are you going to do with me?'

'Provide you with some appropriate accommodation while I decide what should be done.'

He led the boy out into the lane running around the base of the keep and, taking him firmly by the arm, guided him to the right. The weak sun had hardly begun to warm the air and the frost still lurked in the shadow of the walls. Bullock almost danced along the lane, the cold of the ground penetrating the thin soles of his footwear. He pulled the frightened student to a halt at a low archway in the curtain of the keep wall. Peering through it, Hugh could discern a short passage closed off by a heavy, studded door.

'What's this?'

'My lock-up. Perfect accommodation for a desperate murderer, don't you think?'

Hugh would have hung back, but Bullock's firm grip on his arm prevented it. He was thrust forward until the weight of Bullock's body pressed him against the door of the cell. The studs gouged uncomfortably into his chest, making him gasp. The constable was impervious to his pain, only leaning harder against him to reach past and unlock the door with the heavy keys in his great fist. He had clearly perfected this manoeuvre with other, more robust evildoers. As the door gave inwards, the pressure of Bullock's body made Hugh tumble forward into the cell. He fell on to his knees in a pile of old straw that stank of urine. The door was quickly slammed behind him with alarming finality, and he was left alone in the dark.

*   *   *

Rabbi Jehozadok led them into a room piled with books. Falconer and Hannah had been there before, but it filled Thomas with awe. He could not believe so many books existed. The old man turned to his guests and motioned for them to sit down. When they were seated Hannah explained the situation and gently put the leaf into the rabbi's hand. He went over to the hearth and leaned against the heavy stone arch. The fire played redly over his long white beard, and when he turned to face his audience there was a redness in his eyes, too.

'Joshua has much to forget. As a little child he lived with his parents, Isaac and Belassez, in the Jewish quarter in Amiens. They were wealthy, and apparently a happy family. Joshua was doted on by his parents, at two years a solemn baby who they both thought would grow up to be a rabbi. But I suppose a wealthy Jew is a provocation to some . . .'

Jehozadok hesitated, and in deference to his audience avoided saying the word 'Christians'. He continued.

'Some people. When the child of a local merchant disappeared, it was claimed that Isaac had, with the connivance of his wife, tortured and crucified the boy. I can see from your looks that it strikes a chord. I am afraid it is a common crime laid at our door. In this case it went further – perhaps one evil deed was not thought enough for such a wealthy man. The deaths of three other boys over the previous year were laid at Isaac's door. The whole family were dragged to prison and Joshua witnessed the torture of his parents. I will spare you the detail that he has poured out to me.'

Thomas could no longer look into the anguished face of the old man, and turned away in shame at all the stories told by his father that he had believed. Out of the corner of his eye he saw Hannah where she huddled in the darkest corner of the room. She was trembling, and it occurred to him that she and all those like her lived in daily fear of such events being visited upon them. Jehozadok took a deep breath and continued.

'I am afraid that Belassez could not bear the pain. Or perhaps she could not bear to see the evils inflicted on her husband. Anyway she chose to confess to all the crimes, hoping perhaps for some respite from the torture. For her persecutors that was not enough and a promise to convert to Christianity the following day was wrung from her poor lips. The official story then goes that Isaac was so enraged at Belassez's conversion that he slew her in the cell that night then took his own life. The truth was that they were dispatched by the prison guard in a drunken rage.'

'And Joshua – how did he escape?'

'The guard was sober enough to realize that the baby was a valuable commodity. He sold his safety to another Jewish family who brought him to England. You see Joshua is haunted by the torture and murder of his parents, all carried out before his two-year-old eyes. He is plagued by nightmares and sometimes needs relief.'

The rabbi let the leaf drop from his fingers and spiral into the flames, where it sizzled briefly and was gone.

'Where is Joshua now?'

Falconer's question roused everyone out of the silence imposed by the telling of the unfortunate youth's story. Jehozadok stroked his beard thoughtfully.

'Why do you want to know?'

'If he was present in the kitchen that afternoon, perhaps he saw something that might help us find my imaginary Devil.'

The old man paused, then admitted he did not know where Joshua was. Indeed he had not been seen since Samson had sent the youth to the chancellor's cook with the herbs and spices he required urgently. Joshua had not returned home the night before.

'But that is not unusual if he was chewing khat. He might not even know where he is himself until he recovers.'

'Nor know what he had done?' enquired Falconer gently.

Hannah began to protest Joshua's innocence, but the rabbi stopped her with his raised palm.

'Our friend, Falconer, is only asking the obvious question. And I cannot answer it except to say my heart cannot believe he would kill.'

Thomas thought of the stranglehold Joshua had had on him when they struggled on the brink of the half-built tower of St Mary's, and had a mind to refute that. But looking at Hannah, who was imploring him with her eyes to believe in Joshua's innocence, he maintained his silence. Falconer, however, persevered.

'But under the effects of the leaf, he might behave . . . unnaturally?'

Jehozadok sighed and nodded. The Master chose to leave that line of questioning there.

'There is something else you can help me with, knowing your love of old texts.'

He drew from his pouch the torn book cover he had removed from Fyssh's dead but grasping fingers and passed it to Jehozadok. He turned it over in his hands, a flat board covered in red leather with a bare few pages attached. As he peered closely at the few pages with some text, a voice behind Falconer said excitedly,

'I know what it is.'

It was Hannah who had spoken, and now she turned to Thomas, pointing at the torn book.

'Look, it is Margaret's book, Thomas. There is that blood stain on the inside.'

It was Thomas's turn to be excited now, snatching the cover from Jehozadok's grasp.

'She's right, Master. I am sure it's the same book. Or at least what's left of it. But Master Bonham told you he had burned it.'

'It certainly proves one thing,' murmured Falconer. 'Fyssh could not have killed Margaret. If the reason for her death was that the murderer wanted the book back, or the knowledge of its ownership lost, he would not have been waving it around in the cellar last night. No, he was threatening the killer with exposure. But why the book is so important escapes me.'

'I think I can explain that, my friend,' interrupted the sage Jehozadok. 'Unless I am mistaken, that is the beginning of a Cathar Bible.'

Thomas and Hannah looked puzzled.

'A version of your Christian faith declared heretical.'

Bullock was nervous. His squat figure and bent back seemed out of place in the rich quarters of the chancellor of the university. That old fool, Halegod, whose family was no better than his own, had even looked down his nose when the constable asked to see the chancellor. His stubborn persistence had at last forced the old man to fetch his master. In the meantime, Bullock examined his surroundings. To his eyes the brightly coloured drapes depicting hunting scenes hanging against the yellow stone walls were the height of opulence. Falconer had told him that the chancellor was an ascetic, and then had explained what that meant, embarrassed at confusing the town constable with unfamiliar words. Bullock was sure that he understood what the word ascetic meant and this was not it.

'What is it? I do not have much time.'

Bullock turned to face the chancellor, already garbed in his richest robes. No doubt in order to meet with Prince Edward again. In contrast the man's face was ashen and dark rings circled his eyes. The chancellor had obviously had a sleepless night, or had drunk too much of his best wine at the banquet. Perhaps both.

Bullock came immediately to the point.

'I have a student who claims he killed your Master Fyssh.'

'And did he?'

Bullock was startled by the directness of the question. He had expected de Cantilupe simply to insist on the freeing of the student. The university jealously guarded its independence from the town authorities.

'Well?'

'I think not. He is, well, too soft for such a deed.'

'Then what is your problem? Release him.'

'I am afraid if I do that I will shortly be dragging his body from the river.' Bullock could be equally blunt.

'I see.' The chancellor paused, his eyes downcast.

'In whose hall does this poor unfortunate stay?'

'Master Falconer's.'

At that de Cantilupe's eyes brightened, and a smile crossed his lips.

'Then I insist you place the boy immediately in Master Falconer's care. And tell him that I am entrusting the boy's life to him.'

He took Bullock by the arm and hustled him towards the archway and out. Bullock therefore missed the final statement.

'That should keep him out of my hair.'

* * *

The day was cold, but unusually bright, and the sun sparkled off the hoar-frost before it began to melt. Thomas hurried to keep up with the strides of the long-legged Falconer. In the shadow of the new tower of St Mary's the ridged ground splintered under their feet, and Thomas glanced nervously up. Workmen were swinging from the scaffolding, lashing new poles into the place where Joshua had plunged through. It somehow did not seem so high in daylight, but he still marvelled that Joshua had survived. The stonemasons were clearly glad to have a break in the weather and were industriously hoisting large blocks to the top of the tower. The crude pulleys creaked ominously, but the men were glad of the hot work, and strained at the ropes.

'Why does watching other people work attract the young so?'

There was more than a touch of irony in Falconer's voice, and Thomas suddenly realized the Master was yards ahead. Hands on hips he was squinting into the sun facing the laggardly Thomas.

'Perhaps you would prefer to leave this meeting with Master Bonham to me and return to the hall and your studies?'

Thomas protested and hurried to Falconer's side. He did not wish to miss the confession of the little grey man, whom he had suspected all along. The existence of at least part of the book that Bonham had claimed to burn after stealing it from Thomas must proclaim his guilt. Master Fyssh must have found it and, knowing it for a book belonging to the murdered Margaret Gebetz, used it to torment Bonham. That provided a reason for Bonham to have also killed Fyssh in the cellar that night. Thomas began to think this deductive work was simple once you got the hang of it.

There was no answer to Falconer's insistent knocking on the

sturdy oak of Bonham's door. The Master sighed and was about
to resign himself to waiting, when Thomas dodged in front of
him and turned the handle. The door gave to his push, and he
looked eagerly at Falconer.

'This is becoming a habit for you,' groaned Falconer.
'However . . .'

He squinted both ways down the lane and pushed Thomas
ahead of him through the door. Once in he closed it
silently behind him, alert for any sound from the lodgings.
Immediately in front of them a cramped wooden staircase
twisted to the upper floor. The rickety steps did not hold
any promise of keeping silent under his heavy tread. He
motioned Thomas to go and check upstairs, signalling that
he would try the door at the end of the passage he knew
led to Bonham's cramped study. He watched Thomas tiptoe
up the stairs and round the twist in the flight, then went
to press his ear to the study door. It was partially open,
and Falconer fumbled in his pouch until he found his
eye-lenses. He held them up and peered through the crack.
He could see the familiar jumble of books, and one large
tome on one end of the table. He could not hear anything,
but if Bonham was beside the fireplace, beyond the range
of his view, he might have some difficulty explaining this
unorthodox arrival. He pushed the door gently with his bony
fist, and the arc of his vision widened. There was no one
in the room. He swiftly crossed to the table and examined
the book that lay open. It was the Arab, Avicenna's, medical
work, Qanun. Falconer had never before seen such a good
copy. He resisted the temptation to scan it further.

There was still no sound in the house – Falconer could not
even hear Thomas upstairs. The way the book was opened, it
was as though Bonham had only just left the house. But neither

Falconer nor Thomas had seen him in the lane. So where was he? Leaving the study, Falconer was aware of a faintly unpleasant smell, and peered into the shadows under the stairs from where it seemed to come. There was a wooden door, slightly ajar, under the bend of the stairs. Falconer pushed it gently and could see a flight of steps leading down to a cellar. The smell was stronger, reminding him of the butchers' quarter of Oxford. He shuddered at the thought, and at his discovery the last time he descended into a cellar.

Peering around the banisters of the winding stairs, he hissed out Thomas's name. There was no response, and Falconer cursed the inattentive boy. He would have to proceed on his own. He pushed the cellar door wide open and felt his way down the steps in the semi-gloom. There was no handrail and he slid his hands down the walls. They were cold and damp to the touch. The unpleasant smell made him suddenly imagine he was descending into a grave, and he had to stop and steady his nerve. Next thing he would be imagining the Devil again, and without the help of a drug. He smiled at his foolishness and continued down the steps.

There was a turn at the bottom of the steps, so he could see nothing but a blank wall. But the light of a candle flickered on the wall accentuating the uneven brickwork that held back the cold earth. Someone or something was in the cellar, and it stank. At the foot of the stairs, Falconer cautiously peered around the buttress. At first there just seemed to be a jumble of rags spread on a table, puzzling Falconer. He held the eye-lenses up to his face and the scene sprang into focus, and he gasped.

It was truly a scene from hell. On the table lay a naked body, but how it had met its end was impossible to tell. The torso was split from neck to privates and the flesh flayed back in two great flaps. The innards had been scooped out and were spread on the table around the corpse in purple and grey mounds. The stench was appalling and flies hovered and crawled over the gory mess. Falconer held the sleeve of his gown to his nose and approached the abomination. One hand of the man – at least he could still tell it was a man – was flayed to reveal muscle and bone, and was pinned to the table with a nail. Almost gagging, Falconer turned away and was confronted by the figure of the little grey Master standing at the bottom of the stairs, a large and bloody knife in his hand. Wriggling in his clutches, a hand held firm over his mouth, was the unfortunate Thomas.

Chapter Thirteen

Falconer knew this was going to be difficult. Bonham had a secret he could not possibly allow to be revealed. Falconer now knew it, and he could not hide it from the boy. Thomas's eyes fell on the body on the table and his face turned chalky white. He stopped struggling and went almost limp in the little man's firm grasp, all fight gone. Bonham stood as if transfixed, not knowing what to do next. Gently, Falconer tried to resolve the impasse.

'I am sorry to have disturbed you in this way. We should have announced our presence,' he began conversationally, as though he and his student had merely dropped in on Bonham to discuss some text of Plato. 'I should not have let my curiosity get the better of me. It was unforgivable. Thomas, we should leave.'

Thomas's eyes revealed his astonishment at Falconer's calm manner, but Bonham's hand still stopped his mouth. Falconer edged past the table and waved his hand desultorily at the mess.

'This is of no importance after all. Oh, by the way . . .'

He delved casually into his pouch and produced the little knife he had taken from Bonham's drawer the other day. Bonham tensed and Thomas flinched in his grasp. The knife was laid on the bloodied table-top and Falconer continued.

'When I borrowed this I knew, you see.'

To Thomas's surprise, Bonham relinquished his hold on the boy and sighed.

'I suppose I will have to trust you,' said Bonham, lowering his own knife.

Thomas could not believe it – his Master had made a pact with this murderer – and looked from one man to the other.

'But what about the boy?'

'Oh, he still thinks you are a murderer. So the truth will appear as nothing to him. Thomas, take a closer look at the face of the corpse.'

Thomas flinched but did as he was told, with curiosity. Trying not to take in the mound of vital organs spread around, which he could hardly believe could come from one body, he crossed to the table. The head was turned away from him, and, gagging, he leaned over the body and gasped in recognition.

'Isn't it . . . ?'

'Indeed. Young master Moulcom, who already died some days ago, and therefore could not be killed again today.'

'But how——?'

'Really, you must learn to frame your questions properly, Thomas.'

Falconer explained that, after he had taken the knife and realized it was a surgeon's blade, he had suspected Bonham's true secret. The butcher he had seen at work in the town using the same sort of blade helped. And the confirmation came from the many texts in Bonham's study, including the medical one of Avicenna's.

'You see, Master Bonham is purely interested in the science of the body. And as any good scientist will, he wishes to confirm theory with observation. No lesser man than Friar Bacon recommended this approach, and I agree with it.'

Thomas still looked puzzled, and continued to gaze suspiciously at Bonham.

'By dissection of a corpse, Master Bonham seeks to verify the matters propounded by Avicenna on the structure and workings of the human body. Unfortunately less enlightened people, and the Church, disapprove of such activity. Master Bonham would be in great trouble if his little secret were known. As scientists ourselves, we will ensure no such trouble occurs.'

Falconer's firm grip on Thomas's shoulders left him in no doubt as to what he expected of the boy.

Bullock was having difficulty finding Master Falconer to inform him of the chancellor's wishes. At Aristotle's some students said he had gone into Jewry. Bullock had few contacts amongst the Jews – he thought them guilty of arcane and murderous rituals – and hesitated to follow Falconer there, but his duties required it. His peremptory enquiries led him to the rabbi, only to be told that Falconer and one of his students had gone off in search of a regent master. No name was forthcoming, even though Bullock was sure the rabbi knew, nor was any reason given for this flurry of activity on Falconer's part. Bullock knew his friend well and was sure this was the process leading to one of Falconer's deductive conclusions. He equally knew that Falconer was always more secretive than usual at this time – even their friendship would not be enough to extract the name of a murderer before he was prepared to reveal it.

In the meantime Bullock had the problem of a guilt-ridden youth to deal with. A youth who seemed incapable of murder, but who insisted he had committed one. He was angry that the chancellor of the university had brushed him off so easily. Wasn't this a university problem after all? He growled in annoyance, and lurched down Pennyfarthing Lane to return to his quarters and a good jug of ale. If the university wasn't interested then the boy could rot in his lock-up until he was missed.

*   *   *

Thomas was glad they had all returned to Bonham's study before discussing the book. The presence of Moulcom's eviscerated body was not conducive to clear thought, even though the two Masters seemed unaffected by it. Bonham began in a strange way.

'You found my scalpel on Fyssh's body, I presume?'

Falconer was momentarily confused, then blushed at the truth of how it had come into his possession.

'No, I confess I took it myself when I was last here. Why did you think the lamented Master Fyssh would have it?'

'Because he had been here the morning of the banquet, and I left him alone for a while. As I did you.'

The words were delivered accompanied by a sharp look from the little man, and Falconer cast his gaze to the floor.

'Then at the banquet, he spoke to me and said he had something of mine that would reveal what I was. He said I should meet him in the cellars to recover it. I first came home to check what he might have and discovered one of my knives missing. I thought he had used it to come to the same conclusion as you have. The Church still does not approve of anatomy and I imagined he wanted something in return for keeping my secret. He was an odious man, whom no one will mourn.'

'That is why I saw you in the cellar?' Falconer's question was speculative, as he recalled seeing no more than a tonsured head fleetingly in the shadows. The fact that Bonham confessed to this boded well for the truthfulness of his statements generally. Admitting to being present at the scene of a murder could be the statement of an innocent man. Or a devious and guilty one.

'Yes. But I was far too late. I only heard the screaming from a distance as I returned to the hall, and by the time I had found Fyssh he was dead. No one else was there. Then I heard someone coming, who turned out to be you, and hid. Not well enough it seems.'

The hour was getting late, and Bonham paused to light a candle. The flame flickered on his face and cast huge shadows on the wall of the little room. Thomas thought of him poised over the body of Moulcom, drawing his knife from neck to groin, and he crossed his arms in involuntary self-defence.

'Master, the book,' he prompted.

'I had not forgotten, Thomas.'

It was Bonham's turn to be puzzled, or so it seemed.

'Book? What book?'

'The book you took from young Thomas here. The one you said you had burned.'

'And so I did.'

'Then how is it that the cover was found clutched in Fyssh's hand at his death?'

Bonham blanched and leapt across the room, not to the stack of books Thomas had examined on his first visit, but to a dark and battered oak seat with a panelled front. Thomas had sat on it during his search for the book. The seat was hinged and Bonham lifted it and groped inside.

'It's gone.'

'I have the cover here.' Falconer produced the tattered cover with its few pages attached and waved it under Bonham's nose.

'And do not tell me that this is not the same book. Two people have identified it, including Thomas.'

His bald head bobbing, Bonham agreed that what Falconer held was the book. He explained that he was so interested in the contents of the book that he wished to retain it, and had been reluctant to admit to Falconer that it still existed. He had said the first thing that came into his head when questioned by Falconer earlier.

'You see, I found the contents fascinating. I had heard talk of such a work, but never seen one.'

'A Cathar Bible, you mean?'

Bonham was deflated by the fact that Falconer already knew about the book. He was, however, somewhat mollified when he was asked to tell what he knew of the heresy. He explained that Catharism was a French doctrine that supposed two opposing principles of good and evil resided in the spiritual world and the terrestrial world respectively. Souls banished from Heaven resided in fleshly bodies and transferred at death to an animal or another human, depending on the goodness of the dead being. The elite of the sect refused to eat the flesh of beasts as this would interfere with the transmission of souls. He continued, 'The only right path for the heretics is not to associate carnally with women. In this way all souls will eventually return to Heaven as there will be no bodies for them to inhabit.'

Bonham broke off his lecture and shook his head in disapproval.

'This elite – the priesthood – do they have a name?' Falconer already had an inkling of what Bonham would say.

'Oh yes, they call themselves Perfecti.'

Falconer was disappointed. Then Bonham continued.

'Though some go by the name of Bonhommes.'

With the death of Jack Moulcom, the chancellor had not only lost his spy in the Northern Nation of students, but also his doer of deeds that must not be traced back to himself. He now needed someone else to manipulate. De Cantilupe disliked dealing with the fastidious de Stepyng, but it was clear to him they were on the same side in the growing conflict brewing outside the walls of Oxford. His reaction at the banquet made that obvious. The chancellor had dealt diplomatically with

Prince Edward, who still resided temporarily in King's hall outside the town walls. But his real sympathies lay with Earl Simon de Montfort, or more accurately with the good management of the nation, and that was best in Simon's hands.

He had summoned de Stepyng because he understood the older man also supported Earl Simon and would probably initiate a task of common interest. He sat gazing indifferently at the rich hangings Peter Bullock had viewed with awe earlier. For the chancellor they merely kept the chill from penetrating his bones. The evening was growing darker and colder, and he stirred the logs in the fireplace with his foot. Turning at the sound of Halegod's scurrying feet, he forced a smile to his lips and welcomed the regent master.

'Master Robert, thank you for attending so promptly.'

De Stepyng's sallow face was as taut as ever, his lips stern and his eyes unforgiving.

'I am at your service, chancellor.'

De Cantilupe motioned the other man to a seat at the opposite side of the fire, and there was a momentary pause. Then de Cantilupe outlined his request.

'I believe we have a mutual friend of some considerable power, who needs a favour done. And it could be to both our advantages if it is successful.'

De Stepyng kept his silence, gazing unflinchingly into the flames, and the chancellor knew he could trust him. Not so his servant Halegod, so he continued in lower tones. What he was about to say was not to be bandied around the town. At least not yet.

'These recent murders . . .' He paused, marshalling his thoughts.

'You mean the ones which Falconer is running around trying to solve?'

'Exactly. Might we not say that there is some demonic involvement in them?'

De Stepyng was not sure where the chancellor was proceeding with this idea, and remained guarded.

'What I mean is, could not the Jews be involved?'

Now the regent master could follow the drift of de Cantilupe's thoughts. It was well known that he detested the Jews for theological reasons. Curious, then, that his feelings should match Simon de Montfort's, when the latter's were occasioned by purely economic reasons. De Stepyng had heard from travellers that in Canterbury and other towns Jews had been attacked under cover of the general turmoil in the nation. However in every case the Jews' *archa* which stored the records of all Christians' debts had disappeared.

'It would suit our mutual friend if Falconer discovered that the Jews were the culprits in the murders of the servant girl and Master Fyssh. I will not include the student Moulcom in this as it is likely that one of the people in the town killed him. Let them add that accusation to the others later if they wish.'

The chancellor left unsaid what would be the result of a Jew being found guilty of murder. For the townspeople it would surely not end there.

'And my part in all this?' asked de Stepyng.

'Well, I have to admit that Master Falconer does not exactly pay heed to anything I say. I thought that you could find some way of linking the girl Gebetz and one of the Jewish men. An act of carnal corruption followed by ritual slaughter would be believable, would it not? Of course it would have to be told to Falconer soon. Our mutual friend is most anxious on this matter.'

'I will attend to it immediately.'

*　　*　　*

Falconer's room was a cold and unwelcoming place. The fire had been extinguished and, having rooted into the depths of his storage chest, Falconer could only find one candle. This now burned fitfully, trickling molten wax straight on to the table where it stood. Falconer thought he now had all but the key fact in his rag-bag of information, indeed he knew who had killed Margaret Gebetz, Jack Moulcom and Master John Fyssh. But not precisely why, and that irritated him.

Thomas entered with a poor tray of food left over from the supper taken earlier by the other students in Aristotle's hall. There was some cheese and dry bread and the dregs of the large jug of ale that had lubricated the young throats to bouts of song. Falconer could even now hear some loud voices drifting up from the hall below, praising youthful vigour and the futility of age.

> *'Congaudentes ludite,*
> *Choros simul ducite!*
> *Juvenes sunt lepidi,*
> *Senes sunt decrepiti.'*

The singing was drowned in a roar of laughter and Falconer felt even more lost and adrift. Time was that he would be down there with his students, enjoying their youthful energy and ensuring they did not get too carried away. Now his brain was so addled he could not solve a simple problem. He suddenly realized Thomas was pushing the platter of food towards him, and looking expectantly at the regent master. Why did he seem to create this aura of infallibility with the young? Some even considered him a necromancer, merely because of this simple ability to deduce.

'Shall we use dice?'

'Sorry?'

'No matter,' Falconer sighed. 'Let us review the truths we do know. The girl Margaret Gebetz was killed by someone she knew. Because of a book she had.'

'Or had taken from that someone.'

Falconer ignored the interruption.

'Master Fyssh was killed because of a book he had.'

Thomas eagerly opened his mouth to speak, but Falconer held up his finger in admonition, and continued.

'The book was one and the same – a heretic's Bible.'

Thomas managed a question. 'Why was Jack Moulcom killed? What connection did he have with the book?'

'Jack Moulcom was Jack Moulcom.'

Thomas opened his mouth to question this statement of the obvious. But again Falconer stopped his flow, warming anew to his task.

'It's well known that Moulcom ran all sorts of nefarious errands for Masters and merchants alike. Nothing was beneath him, if money was involved. I would guess he acted for our killer in the search for the book which—'

'Margaret had taken.'

'Which the girl had taken, and he knew more than it was safe for him to know.'

What Falconer could not understand was why the possession of the book was so incriminating. No one could accuse the owner of the book of actually being a heretic. These were liberal times and many strange texts were owned by scholars. What was so important at this time and in this city that made the knowledge of Catharism a danger? Once again he reviewed known truths.

'If the reason for the deaths has something to do with France, there are several people in the university with strong connections to that country. It was there that Fyssh, of course, came across Margaret. The chancellor has lectured at the University of Paris, where Bonham has studied.'

'Whereas I have no connection with France at all.' The sharp, precise voice of de Stepyng cut into Falconer's thoughts. He looked up to see the man in his doorway, his hawk-like nose jutting out of his severe face. He wondered how long he had been standing there, and how much deduction he had followed. The man continued, ignoring the presence of Thomas.

'You miss out another connection.'

'And that is what?'

'I have heard that the young Jew who lives with Rabbi Jehozadok was brought here from France as a child.'

'So I believe.'

'Surely it is more likely that if, for whatever reason, you connect the murders with France, and I will not enquire why . . .'

Good, thought Falconer, he did not hear us talking of the Cathar Bible.

'. . . I would have thought it more profitable to suspect the Jew than reputable men such as the chancellor and Master Bonham.'

Falconer snorted at this biased assumption. Widespread hatred of the Jews was not a truth to be added to his deductive process, and he told de Stepyng so.

'Then use this truth, that I have discovered myself. This Jew was seen by several students hanging around Beke's Inn and following the servant girl every time she ran an errand. The talk was that he used her, and made her with child. No doubt he killed her because of that.'

With this he turned and swept out of the room, a self-satisfied smile on his lips. Thomas watched him go, then turned back to face Falconer. He was fearful of what this latest piece of information would do to Hannah. Falconer had a smile of satisfaction on his face.

'Good. We have just received a most valuable fact. Wait here.'

He swept out of the room, too, leaving a worried Thomas in his wake.

De Stepyng was not sure that the seed sown in Falconer's head would come to fruition. The man went off on such tangents he could not be relied on to follow the obvious track. That was why, upon leaving Aristotle's hall, he hurried through the dusk towards Peter Bullock's rooms. He despised the squat, ugly man for his lack of intelligence, but knew that would work in his favour on this occasion. An accusation against the Jews would find fertile ground there, and circulate around the townspeople immediately. After that there would no doubt be indiscriminate attacks on the Jewish quarter. And wasn't that what de Cantilupe wanted?

He left Peter Bullock puzzling over what he had just been told. The scholar was wrong to think that the constable lacked intelligence. Blinded by the man's unprepossessing appearance, he failed to see the qualities that Falconer found manifest. And even if he had known how well Bullock performed his job, he would have put it down to low cunning, no doubt. But despite his own mistrust of the Jews, Bullock did not immediately take de Stepyng at his word. More than ever he wanted to find Falconer and seek advice on this latest riddle. The insistent knocking at his door roused him from his thoughts, and he was amazed on opening it to find the very Master he had been thinking of standing in the doorway. Not for the first time he wondered if Falconer were some magician, who divined people's thoughts.

'Bullock, my friend, I have a request to make of you, but I would rather not make it on the public highway.'

Bullock apologized and stood aside to let Falconer in, and realized that behind his bulk stood another Master of the university. A small grey man, with a sober face, who was unknown to him.

'Forgive me. This is Master Bonham and he has come to assist me on my errand.'

Bonham pulled a face at Falconer's mention of his errand. Clearly he was anxious about something, though carried along by Falconer's enthusiasm. As many people were, in the heat of the moment. Bullock himself knew what it was like to do Falconer's bidding only to look back later and wonder how he could have agreed to it. He hoped this was not another of those occasions. He followed the two Masters into his cramped and dishevelled room, and opened his mouth to broach the subject of the Jews. But Falconer held up his hand.

'Later. I need to secure some information urgently and require your help. Margaret Gebetz, where is she?'

Bullock was not given to whimsical retorts, and forebore from suggesting either Heaven or hell.

'I imagine you mean her body. It is in a box in the crypt of St Frideswide's. I fear there is no one to bury her, so it is as well that the weather is cold.'

Far from being angry at the poor girl's fate, Falconer was much cheered.

'Excellent. I had imagined that I would have to prevail on you to dig her up.'

'Dig her up?' Bullock was shocked. It clearly was one of those occasions he feared, and he was determined not to be led by Falconer into something monstrous.

*   *   *

With such resolve, Bullock was bewildered to be shortly leading the two regent masters down into the crypt of the church where the girl's body had first been brought. Falconer had swept him along again.

All three men's breath coalesced into white plumes in the wintery chill of the crypt. At the bottom of the steps, Bullock held out his lantern to light their way. The dark seemed to press the yellow glow back on itself, and the men could barely see a few paces ahead of them. The heavy pillars that held the weight of the church above seemed compressed into the packed earth that formed the floor of the crypt. They bent their heads low to avoid the arches. Perhaps the whole building was sinking into the earth.

'Here it is.' Bullock pointed at a long coffin of cheap wood pushed in one corner. There was a patina of frost on it, glistening in the light from his lantern. At least the body would not have decayed too much.

Falconer strode over, calling for Bullock to bring the light nearer, and leaned over the box. He grasped the edge on the far side of the coffin with his massive hands and wrenched the lid back. Fortunately the nails were poor and with a squeal that sent a shiver through Bullock the lid came free. Bonham stepped forward and produced a leather roll tied in the middle from his gown.

'What are you going to do?' asked Bullock, half afraid of what he might be told.

'Be quiet and bring the lantern closer,' hissed the little grey Master. He unrolled his leather parcel and laid it out on the lid of the coffin, now lying on the ground. Bullock realized that the parcel held a clutter of knives.

'No! You can't do this. It's blasphemy,' he gasped.

'You are telling me, a regent master of the University of

166

Oxford, what constitutes blasphemy,' snarled Bonham. 'And hold that light still.'

Bullock was about to retort when his friend Falconer grasped his arm tightly.

'Believe me, Peter. It is vital.' His piercing eyes convinced the constable he had to go through with it.

'Very well. But I want no part of it.' He thrust the lamp at Falconer and retreated to the gloom, leaning on a pillar and turning away from what was to happen.

Bonham sighed with exasperation and selected a small knife from the array at his side. Over the stomach of the dead girl he cut through the cloth first, still stiff with dried blood. Revealing the blue-grey flesh beneath, he cut through that as though it were no more than another layer of cloth. With no blood to seep out, Falconer himself could not quite believe it was a human body that Bonham was cutting into. Having made two incisions, he peeled back the frozen flesh and plunged his hands into the girl's abdomen. Feeling around, he pulled up what he sought and cut away again.

'There's your answer, Falconer.' Bonham leaned back and rubbed his hands clean in the dry earth.

Falconer brought the lantern lower and looked at the other man's handiwork.

'It is just as I thought.'

Chapter Fourteen

Thomas de Cantilupe had eyes on greater preferment. His desire was to be Chancellor of all England. With this in mind he was now paying court to the very man whom he hoped could do that for him. In his sumptuous rooms, belying his image as an ascetic he spoke to the man who could be the next ruler of England. Strangely, that man was not so certain himself that he wished to be so.

Seated on the opposite side of the table from de Cantilupe, the remains of a meal spread between them, the man shifted his large frame in the heavily carved chair. His clothes were drab, betraying no indication of his identity, yet fitted his muscular frame well. Well beyond his fiftieth year, he was still imposing and virile with a full head of iron-grey hair. However his handsome face, bronzed through many a campaign, seemed tired and drawn. The Earl of Leicester was a man of paradoxes, unable to quite convince himself that he wanted to overthrow the crown. And yet happy to use the ultimate power of sovereignty for his own ends. It seemed he now wanted to talk to Prince Edward. Indeed he had ridden all the way from Kenilworth after learning that the prince had stopped off at Oxford on returning from the Welsh Marches. He had arrived unannounced with only two trusted men-at-arms to protect him. And all this despite a barely mended leg, which some weeks earlier he had broken in a fall.

De Cantilupe realized the man was still uncertain about

removing both King Henry and his offspring. Even though Edward had, barely days before, broken a truce with Earl Simon's own son, he thought he could make accommodations with him. The earl wanted de Cantilupe to arrange a meeting with Edward, still ensconced in King's hall. This suited the ambitions of de Cantilupe, who would be seen by both sides in the conflict as an arbiter. Much as he might wish Earl Simon de Montfort success, his own ambition demanded he be on the winning side. Whichever it might be.

He poured more wine for the earl and listened as the older man spoke.

'I must achieve this meeting with all secrecy. No one must know it has happened. The safety of England may depend on that.'

'I will myself act as intermediary, and can assure you that no one else will know you were even in Oxford. Except for your men-at-arms of course.'

De Montfort looked sharply at the chancellor.

'I can trust them. I must still learn if I can trust you.'

De Cantilupe flushed, but bowed his head in acknowledgement of the rebuke. Having left the chancellor in no doubt as to who was in control, de Montfort proceeded to win him over by sharing confidences. He sighed deeply.

'Forgive me. If I seem a little over-cautious, it is because strange things have happened to my family since my father led the Crusade against the Cathar heretics in France. My brothers have all three died mysterious deaths, and it is my habit of many years to be distrustful.'

De Cantilupe was mollified.

'My servant doesn't know who you are. And if you keep to your quarters, he will not have chance to assuage his curiosity.'

'Good. Then I will take the opportunity to catch up on my sleep.'

Thomas still was not sure he had taken the right steps. There was pleasure in sitting with Hannah in the tiny back room of Samson's apothecary. But what he had to tell her was of no pleasure, and he did not quite know whether he should be doing it. After Falconer had left him, he had come straight to search out Hannah yet again on an impulse. He blushed to think of the real motive he had for communicating with her. If he needed someone to reason with, then there were fellow students aplenty to talk to. Nor did he really care what happened to Joshua, who had, after all, tried to kill him. No, it was Hannah's approval he sought, and merely being able to be close to her. For a boy brought up in the rude context of a farm, he was now curiously diffident with this strange and self-willed girl.

But he was now committed to his task. Hannah listened carefully, her ivory brow furrowed in a frown and her full lips pursed, as Thomas explained that suspicion for the murder of Margaret was turning towards Joshua.

'Then I must warn him immediately. Some people don't even need the suspicion of a misdeed to persecute us.'

Thomas flushed again at the thought of his own attitude to Jews of only a few days ago, and bowed his head. She tentatively touched his hand.

'And there are those who only see another human being in need,' she said gently. He looked up expectantly, but she was already hurrying out of the room to pass on the warning to Joshua. All Thomas had to do now was to face the possible wrath of his Master.

If that was to come, it would be soon. For almost as soon

as Hannah had slipped out of the back of the room, Thomas heard Falconer's voice in the adjoining area where all Samson's remedies were prepared. He thought it politic not to betray his presence for the moment and squeezed back behind the large wing of the bench on which he sat.

Edward Skepwyth and John Samon were both Northerners and drinking companions. They had studied hard and decided to forego their supper for an afternoon of drinking. They resented the ascendancy of the Southerners at the university, and had fallen to talking about the Black Congregation and the chancellor bowing the knee before Prince Edward at the recent banquet. Like many of their fellows they supported the baronial cause and Simon de Montfort in particular. When another of their friends, Stephen de Hedon, arrived at the tavern in the late afternoon, they were drunk on the cheap and potent brew served there. The landlord was not one to water his ale, and they were frequent customers.

Stephen soon downed the remains of their jug, called for more, and proceeded to tell them of the sight he had seen on his way to the tavern. Leaving Cat hall, where he lodged, he had been passed by no less than the chancellor of the university accompanied by three men. They had been hurrying along, no doubt on an errand of some secrecy. Stephen had not been able to identify the three other men, who had been dressed in ordinary soldiers' clothes. But he knew the chancellor, having only recently been before his court for beating a Welsh student who abused him. He had watched them leave the city by Smith Gate at the end of Cat Street.

'He would have been on his way to fawn over Edward again no doubt,' declared John Samon.

All three were consumed with anger over this apparent

support for the King on de Cantilupe's part, unaware that one of the three ordinary soldiers had been Earl Simon himself. The drink fuelled their anger and, as the afternoon wore on, they resolved to collect some like-minded friends and show that they were not afraid of Edward – King's son or not.

'It is done.'

Hannah's swift return took Thomas by surprise. He was still straining to hear what Falconer was saying to Samson. She too then heard the regent master's voice, and her mouth set in a determined line. She grabbed Thomas's sleeve and despite his protestations dragged him into the next room. Both men looked up in surprise as Hannah burst in on them. She could not contain her anger.

'It is no good you looking for Joshua now as your scapegoat. He has been warned and will be far from Oxford by now.'

Falconer looked puzzled at the outburst, then saw the hapless boy being dragged along reluctantly by his sleeve.

'Thomas. What have you been saying?'

There was anger in his voice, and Thomas was beginning to regret coming to Jewry.

'He told me that someone fed you a fairytale about Joshua and Margaret, and you believed him.'

'Oh, did I?'

'Don't deny that is why you are here.'

'I am here to collect some facts from my friend, your father. What a pity you are not disciplined enough to discover the truth before acting, Thomas.'

The boy began to protest.

'You said when Master de Stepyng left that he had given you a most valuable fact.'

'And so he did, but I didn't say what that fact was.'

Falconer could see he was rapidly losing everyone else in the room. It rather satisfied his vanity that he could see clearer than most, despite his short sight. But of course he owed it all to the rigour of his Aristotelian training, and he should seek to pass it on.

'Thomas, the fact that Master de Stepyng gave me was that he said he had no connection with France. As for the matter of Joshua's supposed dalliance with Margaret and its inevitable result, Bonham and I tested that out. There was no child.'

Thomas opened his mouth to ask how the truth could have been verified. Then he realized Falconer had included Bonham in his explanation. He thought about the eviscerated Moulcom, lying in Bonham's cellar, and felt sick. He did not think he had the stomach for the Master's empirical science.

'What reason would de Stepyng have to lie to you?'

Hannah snorted. 'The best reason of all, probably.'

Falconer looked long at the girl, for he had come to the same conclusion long ago. Still he said nothing, for the discipline of deductive reasoning required truths not surmise. Sometimes he regretted the demands of logic. But in his mind he began to reorder the truths he had laid out many times before in a rough patchwork. Gradually a clearer picture formed before his eyes. Not a patchwork, but a rich and unbroken tapestry. Except the book still refused to fit. The picture was about to unravel, when another small matter floated up to the fore of his mind. He was unsure of its significance, but asked anyway and afterwards was glad he had.

'Tell me, Samson. The day you gave me my eye-lenses, why was de Stepyng here? What potion did you give him?'

'I do not think I have ever dealt with Master de Stepyng.' Samson looked puzzled. 'Perhaps your eyes deceived you.'

'No, no.' Falconer got impatient. 'Thomas, you saw him. You described him to me, and you have seen him since.'

Thomas nodded vigorously to confirm his Master's statement.

'Then you are both mistaken. I know the man you must have seen – he was collecting some poison for rats distilled from the root of bracken. That is Master Belot.'

With a trembling hand, Falconer drew the bloodied book cover from his pouch and reread the almost illegible family inscription.

'Belot,' he whispered.

Another truth was in place. The tapestry virtually complete.

De Cantilupe was pleased with himself. He had brought together the two most powerful men in the kingdom at the moment. Except for King Henry, and he was a weakling who had dispersed his power to the foreigners who surrounded him. It was no good seeking favour of the King – preferment lay with either his son, Edward, or with Simon de Montfort. And both were now beholden to him as a broker in the dispute that was splitting the nation.

He hugged himself, pressing the hair shirt he wore roughly into his body. Pleased he may be, but he must remember humility in all matters. However his pleasure almost caused him to break out into a jig, and he was only stopped by the gentle cough of Halegod. The chancellor pulled himself together and turned to the doorway in time to see his servant thrust aside by Master de Stepyng. Halegod pulled himself upright and, with as much dignity as he could muster, turned and left, muttering under his breath.

De Stepyng seemed unusually on edge, and, with a wave of his hand, de Cantilupe invited him to speak.

'I thought you might wish to know that the matter of the

Jews is resolved. I have seen with my own eyes Falconer hurrying into Jewry, the fire of truth in his eyes. I also fanned the flames a little with the town constable – a prejudiced man who will serve our purpose.'

The Chancellor watched de Stepyng as he paced up and down, the candle flames flickering on his hatchet-face. He seemed to want something more, and interpreting the man's mood according to his inclinations, guessed that de Stepyng sought some preferment for his actions. This was confirmed by the Master's next question.

'The mutual friend of whom we spoke, for whom action against the Jews would be advantageous, would he hear soon of what I have done?'

De Cantilupe, forgetting all humility, could not forbear the hint of his involvement in affairs of State.

'It so happens I have spoken to him only this afternoon, and he is at this very moment in King's hall . . .'

He stopped himself in time from revealing that Edward also was still there. It did not matter if a regent master knew of the presence of Earl Simon, but he must not reveal the existence of the meeting about which he had been sworn to secrecy. Anyway it was clear that de Stepyng cared nothing about whether Edward was still present, for he now seemed most anxious to leave.

'Forgive me, Chancellor. I have interrupted you at a late hour, and will leave you to your contemplations of humility.'

With that, he left the chancellor to wonder if he had been complimented or mocked.

John Samon, Edward Skepwyth and Stephen de Hedon had split up and were each gathering a group of friends, all keen on causing their own mischief in the turmoil that was England.

Although it had begun as a means of showing the Southerners where the friends' sentiments lay, this had been forgotten in the excitement. Students from the two nations of North and South had aligned themselves with the barons, and the thought of showing Prince Edward their feelings was as intoxicating as the ale most of them had consumed.

The three instigators had arranged to meet outside the schools of arts and from there to sally forth through Smith Gate and to King's hall. It was an inconvenience that the King and his family stayed by tradition outside the walls of the city. However the gate would still be open, even though the hour was getting late. Indeed the hour, and the fact it had given ample time for drinking, meant that the numbers exceeded even John', Edward', or Stephen's expectations. There were soon a hundred or more excited students milling around the end of Schools Street and in the lane that ran the length of the city walls. There would undoubtedly be some fun tonight.

Falconer had decided it was politic to inform the chancellor of his knowledge before confronting de Stepyng. After all, there seemed no rush to imprison the man, probably still unaware that Falconer had divined the truth. On his way to the chancellor's residence with Thomas in tow, he had encountered Peter Bullock. The constable lurched alongside him, at last being able to explain that he had incarcerated Hugh Pett, who had seemed determined to assume the guilt of Fyssh's death. Falconer had cheerfully informed him that the boy could not be responsible, and that if Bullock followed him to the chancellor's residence he would learn who was guilty. In the meantime it would do Hugh no harm to ponder on his sins in solitude.

Thus it was that the Master, his student and the constable arrived at the chancellor's door to barely miss the man they sought. The fussy Halegod seemed more discourteous than usual as he led the group into de Cantilupe's presence. The chamber was cold, which was odd for the comfort-loving chancellor, and lit by only two candles. They illuminated the face of de Cantilupe, who stood at a lectern over a sumptuously illustrated Bible. He was frowning and looked up to ask his visitors about humility.

'It says in Matthew, "Whosoever shall exalt himself shall be abased, and he that shall humble himself shall be exalted." Have I not always striven to follow that in my behaviour?'

Falconer did not have time for the chancellor's fancies, and began to explain that he now knew who had killed Margaret Gebetz, Master Fyssh and no doubt Jack Moulcom. He rushed on in his eagerness, despite the puzzlement showing on de Cantilupe's face, yellow in the candlelight.

'He is, or at least his family was, heretic and Margaret knew of it, coming from the same region of Languedoc where it still has a hold. She obviously fled its influence only to find a Perfectus in Oxford. For some reason this mattered to him here and now enough to kill to keep it secret.'

De Cantilupe raised his hand.

'Wait. What heresy? And who are you accusing?'

'Didn't I say?' Falconer smiled at his own haste. 'It's Robert de Stepyng, and the heresy is Catharism. Though why after all this time it matters, I don't know.'

He stopped as de Cantilupe's face paled in shock.

'I can tell you. It matters to Simon de Montfort, because it was his father who was the leader of the Catharist Crusade in the Languedoc. He thought his family was dogged by the consequences of that. And I have just told de Stepyng where Earl Simon is.'

'Where?'

'He is in King's hall at this very moment. But you will never catch up with de Stepyng now. It is too late.'

His head slumped over the Bible, and his knuckles showed white as he clutched the edges of the page. However it was not in Falconer's nature to give in, when so close to the solution of a mystery. He quickly motioned to Thomas.

'Go to the North Gate and warn the guard. No one must enter or leave, even if they claim to be the King himself.'

Thomas dashed out of the room, almost bowling over the startled Halegod hovering in the doorway.

'We must try to stop him. He may not have gone straight there. Perhaps he has gone back to his rooms for a weapon, or the poison he got from Samson. And if he intends to use poison, he will be working secretively. After all, he has waited this long to be in the right place at the right time.'

He turned to Bullock.

'Have you got the key to Smith Gate?'

Bullock jangled the bunch at his waist.

'I always carry it.'

'Then let's try and head him off and lock him inside the city.'

Halegod knew this time to stand well clear of the doorway as the two left with haste, the bent back of Bullock lumbering alongside the long stride of the Master.

De Stepyng cursed his ill-luck. He had gone from the chancellor's rooms to his own to collect the sweetmeats he had poisoned, even though this meant going out of his way. He had stopped long enough also to reverently finger once again the Bible he had wrenched from Fyssh's dying grasp. It was mutilated – the front cover gone. But with it had gone the stain of his father's blood, splashed on the Bible when the elder Belot

178

had been slaughtered by de Montfort's Crusaders. Somehow it was now almost purified. There only remained one more act to perform. He would stick to the scheme that had been so successful dispatching Amaury de Montfort twenty years before. It had been more subtle than the violent and chancy deaths he had wrought upon the Earl's other two brothers. He did not imagine he would have much success bursting in on Earl Simon with a knife. No, he would be more likely to achieve his purpose by presenting himself as a trusted supporter with something to please Simon's sweet tooth.

As he came up Schools Street, he saw there was a swirling mass of drunken students shouting incoherently to each other. They were going to delay him, and he began to push through them angrily. He soon realized that was a mistake. In their sodden state they were no respecter of his office, and began to jeer and jibe. He was pushed and pulled by the sleeves of his robe, the material tearing as he was buffeted first one way then the other. He tried to back out of the crowd, but suddenly there was a shout from two ringleaders at their head and the whole mob surged forward. De Stepyng was carried along with them.

Thomas too was delayed by the mob of students. But he had stayed on the fringe, trying to decide whether it was better to push through them or detour around them. He realized the press of bodies ahead of him was getting ever tighter, and knew his only hope of getting to North Gate quickly was to go around the pack. He was about to turn down the narrow alley that ran off Schools Street parallel to the city walls, when he thought he saw an older man in the midst of the mob. The man was dressed in the robes of a Master, and suddenly his face, flushed with anger, turned towards Thomas. The hawk-like features told him it was de Stepyng.

Abandoning his mission to North Gate as irrelevant, he began to worm his way through the mass of jostling students towards where he had seen Margaret's killer. The faces around him were red and sweating, their breath laden with ale fumes. Calling encouragement to the ones ahead of them, they pulled Thomas into their midst and surged forward. For what seemed like an age de Stepyng and Thomas bobbed along like two pieces of flotsam on a surging ocean. Now and then Thomas rose on the crest of a wave of bodies to spot de Stepyng, and each time he was slightly nearer. At last he saw that the Master had squeezed himself up against the city walls and was no longer being carried along in the mob. Flailing his arms as though he were swimming, Thomas cut through the crowd of students, and suddenly found himself face to face with de Stepyng. Then it struck him he did not know what he was going to do. Merely getting to de Stepyng had been uppermost in his mind, not how to stop him.

De Stepyng looked piercingly at Thomas, knowing that this blond-haired bumpkin was one of Falconer's band of students, and could tell from the wary look in the boy's eyes that Falconer knew. He grasped him tightly by the arm and pulled him close.

'He knows, doesn't he?'

The boy nodded defiantly, unsure of his fate.

'We will wait until most of these idiots are through the gate, then just stroll through ourselves.'

He pulled Thomas closely up against him, twisting his arm painfully.

'The chaos they are causing may even make it easier for me. No one will be able to get through to King's hall for some time.'

He turned Thomas towards the gate and began to move

along the edge of the crowd. Suddenly he stopped with a gasp and Thomas saw that the surge had stopped, and there were angry cries coming from the head of the mob. Thomas was tall for his age, and could peer over the heads around him to see what had stopped de Stepyng in his tracks. And what angered the mob of students.

The gate was closed, presumably locked because the ring-leaders were rattling the handle and beating on the stout oak. Pressing through the crowd towards them were the figures of Bullock and Falconer. They were finding it slow going, even though Bullock was waving a heavy club. Falconer stopped and raised some device to his eyes, checking where he had last seen de Stepyng and the boy. There was something nightmarish about their progress towards Thomas, and he could not imagine them reaching him in time. Indeed de Stepyng yanked on his arm and began to drag him away. They were in a thinner part of the press and could make better progress. For a moment Thomas lost sight of the other two men and despaired. He began to call for help from the students around him, but without letting go of the boy's arm de Stepyng wrapped his forearm around Thomas's throat stifling his cries. Anyway, the other students were concentrating too much on the efforts to break through the gate to be concerned about a minor squabble in their midst.

Thomas was pulled backwards on to a flight of steps, stumbling as de Stepyng pulled him upwards.

'Stay on your feet,' the man snarled.

Thomas saw they were going up steps cut in the side of the wall, leading to the postern over Smith Gate. Soon they were above the press of jostling bodies, and it was getting dark. Could Falconer or Bullock see them? As he swept his gaze over the crowd, he saw the lumbering figure of Bullock and managed a squawk before de Stepyng stopped his throat again with a savage wrench. Looking down he could see Bullock anxiously casting his gaze around the crowd, and Falconer was shouting and pressing the device to his eyes. They had lost him.

Chapter Fifteen

The din in the lane was deafening, and Falconer had to shout with his face inches from Bullock's to be heard.

'Can you see them? Can you see them?' Anxiety was written all over his features.

'They've just disappeared,' yelled Bullock, his legs spread apart to steady himself in the jostling throng. He was like a rock in a raging sea, and Falconer clung on to his shoulder for safety. He spun round, scanning over the heads of the crowd with his eye-lenses, but could not see them. He groaned.

'The man is mad. He has killed three people in the last few days. We must find him for Thomas's sake.'

'And Earl Simon's.'

Behind them someone had found a stout bench and it was passed over the head of the throng in willing hands. The students nearest the gate began to batter the locked door with it. From elsewhere an axe was found and someone began to swing it at the oak panels.

'They were near the wall when we saw them last. Where could they have gone?'

Bullock suddenly looked upwards at the reinforcement over the gate.

'Of course, the postern. The steps to it are cut into the wall near by.'

He began to thrust his way through the students, careless of the heads he broke with his club.

De Stepyng estimated that by going along the top of the wall to the North Gate, through and then doubling back along Candich outside the walls he could still reach King's hall before Falconer. They would be trapped in the turmoil of the rioting students for a long while yet. He would of course have to rid himself of the boy immediately. If he threw him over the parapet to the back of the mob, his body would not be noticed for some time. Just another foolish student killed in the affray.

He pushed Thomas roughly to the inner edge of the wall and forced his head out over the void. Thomas grabbed at the stone of the parapet, tearing his fingers in a desperate bid to keep his balance. The dark lane below spun in his vision, the bobbing heads of the students oblivious to his plight. De Stepyng released the hold on his throat and grabbed his legs, heaving Thomas off balance. He began to slide down the canted lip of the parapet with nothing to grasp. He locked one knee around the upright stones to his left, and gained some control over his slide. But de Stepyng was using all his force to prise his leg away from his only hold on survival. He began to weaken, his leg slowly being torn from the stone, when suddenly the force was no longer there.

Thomas heard an unearthly squeal and the scuffling of feet. The muscle in his thigh was almost numb with strain, but he pulled himself back from the brink. He slid back over the ridge of the parapet and collapsed to his knees, trembling. Looking up, he saw de Stepyng lurching backwards, clawing at something at his throat. He seemed to have a demon on his back, uttering hellish curses. His sallow face turned red and his eyes bulged in his head as he struggled to release himself from the Devil's clutches.

Thomas saw that it was Joshua hanging on de Stepyng's back, and was for once glad the Jew had been dogging his footsteps. He drew breath to thank him for his assistance, only to realize Joshua's face was a mask of white with blazing eyes. He was clearly drugged. As if in confirmation the Jew hissed into de Stepyng's ear.

'Jew-killer. You won't murder my parents.'

In his maddened state he imagined de Stepyng was his parents' jailor. And this time he was old enough to fight back. He tightened his grip on de Stepyng's throat, his fingers like claws, and screamed again.

'Violator of my mother!'

For himself, de Stepyng had other visions. The demon on his back was a familiar of the terrible knight, who was himself de Montfort incarnate. He swung around in terror, looking for the figure that had haunted his life. He saw him appear by magic over the parapet, dismounted from his horse at last. There was horror in the regent master's eyes, and he crashed backwards against the outer parapet, trying to dislodge Joshua from his shoulders. It didn't work, and he staggered forward to try again. Almost into the arms of the knight, whose form was clad in shining steel, ornately worked in gold. De Stepyng could discern every curlicue that spiralled across his chest. Behind the lattice of the helm there was only darkness. The Master stood transfixed.

Thomas dared not move as the battle between de Stepyng and Joshua seemed poised in time. Neither moved as their efforts seemed to balance out. A ray of light from the sun, setting over his shoulder, flashed on a glass panel in the King's hall outside the city walls. Thomas raised his hand to shade his eyes.

De Stepyng flinched as the deathly knight raised his metal-clad fingers to his helm. The face-plate was raised and revealed nothing but an awful void. Had there never been anything to sate his revenge after all? The screeching demon clawed at his face, tearing the flesh, and blood coursed down his cheek. Lurching backwards to knock it off his shoulders, he thrust not against the wall but the open space of an archery point. He scrabbled hopelessly for balance, but the weight of Joshua on his upper body carried him inexorably backwards. He saw his own father's face in the knight's helmet, lecturing him about how the souls of the wicked were cast over the precipice by demons, and understood.

Thomas saw the utter fear on de Stepyng's face, and the exultation on the mask that was Joshua's. Then they were gone.

On trembling legs Thomas staggered to where they had gone over and peered into the gathering gloom. The two bodies lay motionless at the foot of the wall, and Thomas turned away to face Bullock and Falconer appearing at the top of the steps. At that moment there was a great cheer, and the students burst through Smith Gate into the fields beyond.

The Jewish cemetery outside East Gate was a cold and eerie place to be. The white shroud of mist hung over the group gathered around the graveside. All sound seemed to be deadened, and Thomas was reminded of his first day in Oxford and the unearthly shriek that had started this curious sequence of events. Rabbi Jehozadok was wrapped in a heavy shawl to protect himself from the cold, and he wiped away a tear with the end of it. Samson and Hannah stood either side of him and he put his arms around them for mutual comfort.

'Poor Joshua. He was never happy in life. Perhaps he has found something better now.'

They each thanked Falconer and Thomas, then as a group

walked away into the mist. Thomas looked for a while at Hannah until she disappeared from sight, then turned back to Falconer.

'I still don't understand why you checked de Stepyng's story about Joshua, if you knew he was the killer.'

'I thought he was the killer,' Falconer reminded the boy. 'I already had some truths. De Stepyng said he did not know Margaret, and yet you remember Hannah telling us she had once had to read a message Margaret was delivering for Fyssh?'

'Yes. Margaret had forgotten who it was for, and couldn't read herself.'

'Hannah remembered who it was addressed to – Master de Stepyng. So he must have seen her at least once. Of course that is not conclusive, and I needed more. His not eating at the banquet was curious but not important. Until we established the link with Catharism. Remember Bonham telling us that the Perfecti did not eat meat?'

Thomas shook his head, bewildered.

'Then there was the fact de Stepyng supplied which was more important than the story about Joshua – he said he had no connection with France. Even though his own mother was French.'

Seeing Thomas's look of uncertainty, Falconer reminded him that the chancellor had told them so in de Stepyng's very presence.

'And he did not refute the fact. You see all these truths by themselves are small but, with the name on the book and his purchase of the poison distilled from bracken, supply the greater truth. What angers me, however, is that on the day after the murder of the girl de Stepyng seemed to know her throat had been cut even before the facts were common knowledge. He said as much to me, and I put it from my mind. I might have prevented other needless murders.'

He sighed.

'As for checking his story about Margaret and Joshua – I confess to simple curiosity.'

He saw Thomas had a long way to go to understanding his method and the workings of his inquisitive mind. He patted the boy on the back.

'Come, we have some packing to do.'

Thomas looked puzzled.

'I understand that the King wants to use Oxford as his military base. After the events at Smith Gate, he is not going to want a disloyal student rabble under his feet. I understand we are going to move to Northampton.'

Thomas protested.

'But I've only just got here!'

Epilogue

The events of the student riot at Smith Gate are recorded in history, but the actual reason for the locking of the gate has not been recorded, and is only the subject of surmise on the part of historians.

In March 1264, King Henry did indeed enter Oxford and many students left for Northampton. Perhaps it was predictable then, due to the old warning which boded ill to any king who entered within Oxford's walls, that Henry lost the Battle of Lewes to Simon de Montfort on 14 May of that year.

Simon held sway over a divided nation for fifteen months, before himself being killed and mutilated at the Battle of Evesham. King Henry ruled until his death in 1272, and Edward succeeded him while on Crusade.

Thomas de Cantilupe achieved his ambition, and was appointed Chancellor of England by Earl Simon. In the latter part of his life he was also a close adviser to King Edward.

Richard Bonham died of typhus only a few years after the events described here. It is thought he contracted the disease from an infected body he was anatomizing.

Both Rabbi Jehozadok and the apothecary Samson died of old age and lie buried in the Jewish cemetery next to Joshua. Nothing is known of Hannah, who was expelled along with all the other English Jews in 1290.

Peter Bullock was killed in 1274 in the midst of a pitched battle between Northern and Welsh students. Whilst trying to separate two fighting students, he accidentally stepped in the way of a blow from a rusty sword.

Hugh Pett returned to run his father's estates in Essex when his older brother died during Edward's Crusade in the Holy Land. He married and had three sons.

Thomas Symon returned to Oxford with others from Northampton, and remained there, becoming in his turn a regent master of the Faculty of Arts. He later played a part in the founding of University College.

William Falconer was to have many further adventures, occasioned by his insatiable curiosity. He travelled abroad, corresponding regularly with Thomas Symon, and it is believed he died in what a later traveller would call Cathay and we would call China. It was always his belief that the world was a globe.

Forthcoming Vista paperback crime titles

VISTA